Your Eyes as Honey

Kate Holloway

Copyright © 2022 Kate Holloway

All rights reserved.

ISBN: 9798832234458

DEDICATION

For someone who was going through a very rough time when I wrote this. More bad times may come, but daylight always seeps in.

Dear reader, please be aware this book contains the following: misogyny, sexual assault, abuse, murder. Take care of yourself.

-gracious your form and your eyes as honey:
Desire is poured upon your lovely face
Aphrodite has honored you exceedingly…

-Sappho

CHAPTER 1

The sun is a searing disk in the sky, watching Persephone as she lays in her field of flowers. Her eyes are closed, her breathing even. She is not sleeping, but rather listening. The buzz of bees, conversations among warblers and shrikes, the gentle shush of the creek in the forest. Calendula, Anthemis, and Chrysanthemum tickle her face. The sun soaks into her skin, warming her until she feels like a band of light. Her whole body hums.

She is content for the moment. Although she knows she will have to return to the village, to the empty house her mother had left a day ago. A village a few hours away is having issues with rot in their gardens, and Demeter, the keeper of the harvest, was called upon to help. Demeter invited Persephone to go, but Persephone declined. She would be of no use. She is a goddess's daughter with no godly gifts.

Her mother had always assured her that her gifts would reach their full potential someday when she is grown. But while Persephone grew, her power did not. She has been on the earth for one-and-twenty years now.

She peeks open one eye and squints at a poppy stalk next to her. She takes a deep breath, then concentrates, a crease forming between her eyebrows with the effort. The poppy stands up straighter, grows a quarter of an inch, then stops. Persephone wilts. Closes her eyes once more.

"Feel it, darling. The earth beneath your fingertips, the earth within," her mother would say when instructing her.

Persephone felt something when she tried to use her power, but she wasn't sure if it was the pull of being one with the earth. It felt more like a tugging downward, beneath the dirt and roots. Insistent and impatient, wrapped around her ribs. No matter how hard she tried, she could never heal olive crops or make fennel rupture from the earth as her mother could. She used to weep after her mother's instruction. Demeter would hold her tight until she cried it out, never admonishing, never criticizing, just rocking gently.

"One day, my dear," she would say. "One day."

In the meadow, Persephone stretches her arms above her like a cat. Today will not be 'one day'. She will improve by the time her mother returns, she swears. But perhaps right now she could just take a quick nap. Even from that little bit of magic, she feels exhaustion in her bones. They feel heavy in a satisfactory way, like when she would play hours of tag with the other children in the village. She falls asleep to the song of the larks.

In her dreams, there is a voice. It is a deep, smoky thing that purrs her name in her ear, raising the golden hairs on her arms. So close she can feel the speaker's breath brush the soft skin behind her ear. She doesn't move away. She tries to nuzzle backward into the speaker's chest, but she stumbles against air. There is nothing behind her but forest, moonlight speckling the moss through the leaves. It is cold without the speaker.

"Come back," she whispers, bottom lip trembling. Then she orders it, "Come back!"

There is the lightest brush of fingertips along the small of her back, and she whips back around. No sign of the speaker, but a single seed lies between her feet. She drops to her knees and scoops up the seed. It is a tiny thing, but the air around it is heavy as if the pod has its own little gravity. Persephone does what is in her nature to do. She digs into the earth with her hands, carving a hole just cozy enough. The ends of her fingernails become minuscule, black crescent moons. She drops the seed inside its new home and begins patting and folding the dirt over it. Gently, as if tucking a child in for the night. When it is completely covered, she places her hands palms-down on the earth. She exhales slowly through pursed lips. Then she feels the speaker's warmth once more around her like a phantom embrace, and she closes her eyes. A pleasant hum courses through her veins - a vibration, tumbling, growing, ascending - and then there is clarity. She opens her eyes to see a fully-grown narcissus before her, leaves outstretched as if reaching for her. Her lips curl into a smile, and then she's beaming with all the intensity of a goddess's daughter.

"You know where to find me," the voice is at her ear again. Before she can respond, she is jolted awake.

The sun has moved across the sky enough that she estimates she's slept for about an hour. She still feels the glowing comfort of the dream, though it fades fast when she hears hooves approaching. The voices of men wind through the trees, laughing loudly, jeering.

"Shit," she whispers, stumbling to her feet. She can pick some of the voices out. There is one rising louder than the others. Booming and arrogant. The crown prince Aetius. He is no prince, in her mind. She breaks into a run across the meadow, upsetting the bees resting on their plumes as she rushes through their sanctuary. The flowers pop right back up where she trampled them beneath her feet. They know her as one of their own.

"Persephone!" his voice is a dagger to the pit of her stomach. He's spotted her. The band of guards with him sends their horses into a full gallop. Her legs pump even harder, her lungs feel as if they will split open at any second.

"PERSEPHONE!" Without looking back, she already knows his face is reddening. The hoof beats are catching up with her.

There is a flash of russet in the corner of her vision, then the beast is in front of her, cutting her off so suddenly that she falls back to the ground. She props herself on her elbows, but before she can rise, the four other guards and the prince surround her on their mounts.

The prince jumps down and unsheathes his sword in one swift motion. He aims the jagged blade at her heaving chest. The tip of it barely touches her skin, but she feels its coldness in every limb. She bares her teeth at him.

"One day you'll learn to stop running from me," he seethes. The high sun is behind his head, spinning his blond hair into a gold halo. His eyes are steely, demanding blue. Most girls in the village swoon over him, but to Persephone, he's about as handsome as a wasp.

"What do you want?" she spits out.

"What I always want."

"No."

He smiles. It's the kind of flesh-eating grin that makes Persephone's stomach roil

"You're already halfway there, laying like that." His guards chuckle. She glances at them. Though their faces are hidden by gold-plated helmets, she probably knows them. Probably has visited their mothers for garden troubles.

She tries to get to her feet again, but he presses the blade into her skin enough to cut. A drop of blood winds its way underneath the bust of her dress.

"Let me up," she says.

"Where is your mother, Persephone?" He feigns searching the meadow around them. "It seems she's out of town. And you're here, all alone. Quite literally powerless."

She wills her eyes not to well up, but it is in vain. Tears brim and the edge of her lids. Silently, she focuses on the earth beneath her. Trying to make something happen, anything. Her mother can command wheat to strangle men, tomato vines to crawl into their eyes and down their throats. Persephone has only ever seen her do it once when a band of thieves came upon them during one of their travels. She still has nightmares about it where she is the one being strangled. Persephone's fingers tremble as she grips the blades of grass beneath her. She squeezes her eyes shut, but instead of the hum she should feel, she feels a deep droning crescendo. When it gets to be too much, she opens her eyes once more. The prince is still a shadow over her, smiling that not-smile. The plant life around her has grown maybe a centimeter under her efforts. Heat flames in her cheeks.

"See," Aetius says. "Powerless."

He nudges her knee with his boot, tsking. "You're always so dirty."

Dirt and leaves cling to her dress, and the crown of flowers upon her brow is mussed. There are twigs tangled in her hair as if birds thought she was the perfect home and began constructing while she slept.

"Let me GO, Aetius," she says lowly.

"YOU DON'T GET TO TALK TO ME LIKE THAT," he bellows at her. She flinches back until her back touches one of the guard horse's legs. His face twists in fury. "I am the crown prince. I give the orders."

His sword is raised high in the air now. One swoop and he could slice her throat open. She stays stock still.

One of the guards clears his throat then barks, "You will apologize to his Highness, girl."

She swallows, stares hard at his neck. So white. What color would it turn if she could wrap her hands around it and *squeeze*? Perhaps the sickly purple of vervain petals. Her voice is hoarse when she says, "Forgive me, your majesty. I've forgotten myself."

He visibly deflates, closes his eyes as if counting to ten. He sheathes his sword once more. The ring of metal sliding against metal is sharp in the silence.

"I originally came here to give you good news," he says in deadly calm. He waits for her to respond, but she has no idea how. "It has come time for me to wed."

She stares back at him with wide eyes.

"You will be my wife."

She feels as if the breath has been knocked out of her. She opens her mouth, only to close it once more.

"Our wedding will take place in a month. I expect you to be willing, and to be clean for the dressmakers. Should you try to run, my men will find you, and I will personally oversee your punishment."

She keeps blinking, scowling.

He gets down on one knee. Instead of offering a ring, he leans in so close to her face that his wine breath fans over her cheeks, mixed with horse and body odor.

"You will be obedient." He somehow makes the statement both a promise and a warning.

"Why would you want to marry someone so *powerless* and *dirty*?" she counters.

"Even if you don't have power, I'm sure my heirs will. Perhaps it skips a generation."

"You don't want a wife. You want a broodmare."

"Precisely! How fortunate that we understand each other."

"And what if I can't give you heirs?"

"You will be worthless. And I'll kill you."

"My mother would never let you get away with it."

"You will die in a tragic accident, and your mother will feel pity for her bereaved son-in-law."

"I could tell her, you know. I could tell her everything."

"Tell her what? About how much of a whore you've been? She'd think you're disgusting. She'd think I was doing you a favor by marrying you."

"No she wouldn't. You don't know my mother," she

spits, but fear flares in her chest nonetheless. It's exactly why she hasn't told her mother.

"Ah, but I know mothers. And mothers always want what's best for their daughters, which is always marrying the man with the most power."

"You're delusional."

She should be accustomed to getting slapped by now, she thinks, but the sting of his sweaty palm against her face stuns her still.

She holds her breath until he straightens back up and waves a signal to his guards. They begin to make their way over the meadow, back in the direction they came.

He grips her forearm suddenly, "I'll come by your little hovel at midnight. This is your chance to make your disobedience up to me. I want your hair in two braids."

He releases her arm, hopping up on his horse and making his way to his men ahead.

Persephone swallows the bile in her throat.

CHAPTER 2

The cottage she and her mother share is two stories, filled to the brim with pots of herbs, clumsily sat on windowsills and tables and spare corners. Bound sprigs of lavender hang from the rafters. The hearth is huge and surrounded by cushions and sofas of various assortments. Zymi, the plumpest of their seven cats, always greets Persephone at the door. He takes her chin scratches as his due and emphatically twines around her ankles when she stops.

He follows when she sinks into a chair by the hearth, head in her hands. Head butts her in the shin.

"What am I going to do, Zymi?" Her voice is garbled behind a lump in her throat.

Her hands shake. She feels an invisible layer of grime over her entire body. She knows it's not real, but the feeling comes over her following all interactions with Aetius. She wants to scrub and scrub until her skin is raw and free of the blight he brings.

Zymi stares up at her with his moon eyes.

Something Persephone loves about cats is that they're so extraordinarily intelligent and stupid at the same time, something she feels she has in common with them.

YOUR EYES AS HONEY

"What would you do?" She asks the creature at her feet. He meows back at her. "Good idea." She smiles, though her lip trembles.

When he was younger he would get into fights with neighboring cats, or rather, they would pick a fight with him. Zymi is docile for the most part. But if hurt, Zymi would give as good as he got. He would come back at night licking his wounds with his head held high, seemingly content in the knowledge that his opponent was probably worse off than he.

But if Persephone takes the feline route, she will have no home to return to after the fight. Aetius would ensure she was punished, either by execution or exile or some other horror.

One year ago, the first time he cornered her in an alleyway, she got over her terror of him being the prince and punched him in the face. He had slapped her so hard she saw stars behind her eyes. "I can burn everything you love," he had told her. More than once someone who'd gotten on his bad side had perished in a house fire, or drowning, their families disappeared.

Zymi hops up on her lap and it startles her. Which is enraging. She's tired of jumping, shying away from every man she sees on the street because it may be him, or they may be like him. She's tired of feeling like a prisoner in her own body. She strokes Zymi's fur to calm herself down.

He likes her to have two braids because it's easier to pull, and reminds him of some sickening school maiden fantasy. He'd told her so, without shame.

He says she should at least try to enjoy it, it's going to happen anyway. Plenty of girls like it rough.

She thinks perhaps she would too if he hadn't stolen that choice from her. Now the thought of anyone seeing her naked or touching her makes her want to vomit. Her body feels disgusting. Bathing is hard for her because it means she has to see it, acknowledge it.

Everyone else in the village believes him to be generous

and kind and dignified and heroic. Demeter doesn't trust him, but has been cordial when someone has asked for her help in the castle gardens on the royals' behalf. Persephone thinks her mother likes to play human.

She misses her mother.
She needs her mother.
Her mother isn't here.
There is a pit in her stomach the size of an ocean.

"Should I have told her?" she whispers to Zymi. He gives her his deep, rumbling purr. Even more terrifying than the prospect of being forced to marry Aetius, is her mother hating her. She is not the kind of mother who talks to her daughter about sex. Persephone only learned about it from the titters of other young people in the village, and the way they spoke about it made it clear it was something to be ashamed of. Even if Persephone wanted to tell someone, there's no one to tell who would help her. She wishes she could ask her mother what she should do, without telling her everything. But Demeter is miles and miles away.

But, that means if Aetius were to enact revenge on her for resisting him, he wouldn't be able to hurt her mother. Demeter is strong, but if Aetius brought his whole army against her she's not sure who would come out on top. She could let all the cats outside and run to the woods should he decide to burn the house. Demeter and Persephone can always build another one. That's what women are best at doing, after all. Rebuilding. Surviving.

She bathes and puts on a silk nightgown. It clings to her damp skin as she fumbles around the kitchen. The sun has gone down now, and flames in the fireplace make shadows dance in her periphery. She finds their most jagged knife, made for cutting meat or particularly hard bread loaves, and tucks it under her pillow. In her room, she sits on her bed, looking through the window. Various villagers pass by on their way home from the market or tavern. Some drunkenly laugh with each other, others are solemn, placid. This village has many stories, Persephone thinks. She might become one if she gets the nerve to do what she wants to night.

With each minute that passes the pit of dread in her chest eats her up more and more. But, underneath that blackness, there is a sliver of something else. Something that makes her heart skip a beat, makes her want to dance a heathen dance. Either way, she simultaneously wants Aetius here right now and for him never to arrive.

He does anyway. He ties up his horse in the back and she hears him waltz through the front door, which she hadn't bothered to lock.

"Where are you, field rat?" he calls in a sing-song voice.

"How original," she mutters.

"Do I hear you upstairs?"

She stays silent, perched on the bed. Shoulders back. Chin held high. He comes up the stairs and enters her room, swaying just a bit. He slams the door behind him and gives her a too-wide smile.

"You should answer when I call for you." His words are slurred.

"You should go easy on the wine," she quips back.

That wipes the grin off his face and he stumbles towards her, gripping her face with his hand.

"Maybe I liked it better when you didn't answer. Stop talking back, or I may cut out your tongue."

"How will I say my vows if I cannot speak?"

He shoves her face back and she catches herself on her elbows.

"Where are the braids?" He tries to grab her hair but she dodges him and he almost falls onto the bed, he's so drunk. "I told you two braids."

"Maybe you should lie down," she says.

"Fuck you."

She scoots back when he reaches for the hem of her gown, but he grabs her ankle and yanks her back toward him. In a second, he's pinning her down with his body. One hand grips the hem of her nightgown and pulls it up to her waist. The other knots painfully in her hair.

The old panic sets in and she thrashes, one hand searching for the blade and the other pushing against him. He bites into her shoulder, hard, and she sees red. She slaps him so hard her nails cut lines into his cheek. He's stunned for a moment, she usually isn't this brazen.

Something in his eyes flares.

"I. Am. Your. Prince." he seethes, spittle flying from his mouth. His hands close around her throat at the same time her fingers wrap around the knife's handle. He puts so much force into his grip that she sees black spots within seconds. She musters up all the strength she has and plants the blade into his shoulder.

He screeches, but only presses the column of her throat harder.

Almost everything is black, and something primal in her rises. There is a ringing in her ears getting louder and louder. It reaches a fever pitch and his hands disappear from her throat.

Her chest heaves as she scrambles away and her vision clears. Aetius's mouth is wrenched open in a silent scream. Vines crawl around his throat like his fists around hers. She gasps and they fall away. He collapses on the bed, wheezing. She sees the vines came in through a crack in the window, and they are slowly creeping back out. She backs away one step, then another, and another. Then she runs.

Her vision is blurred by tears and all she can think to do is run, run, run. She bursts through the front door and maneuvers around the few people on the streets, some of them jeering at her in her nightgown. Everything is too close and loud in the city - the fire from torches burn into her retinas and the crowds of voices spilling out of taverns bang against her eardrums. Something is holding on just as tight to her as her fear, constricting in her chest. It is physical light. It is ecstatic. It is alive. She pays no heed to the gravel slicing into the soles of her feet as she flies through the village. She doesn't even stop for a breath when she reaches the forest. She keeps straight on for the meadow - her meadow. She breaks through the tree line and finally slows, bending in the middle of the meadow to catch her breath. Over the gentle shushing of the breeze through the trees, there is a cacophony of men's voices, shouting out indistinguishable phrases. Her lungs feel as though they may burst and when they find her dead body, Aetius will just be angry he didn't get to do it himself. As she bends over, ears pricked, the voices rise. They get louder and louder. Closer. She groans. She hadn't incapacitated him enough - and they're after her far sooner than she thought they'd be. There is a faint flickering in the copse she just ran out of. Torches. She wills her legs to take her farther despite the deep ache in them. The tall grass and wildflowers brush against her calves as if urging her on. She keeps running, out of the meadow and into the deep black forest on the other side. All she can think about is getting away from the town.

She's been running for about ten minutes when her legs begin to tremble. She's growling in frustration as she pushes on, but it feels as if she will never get enough oxygen in her lungs and then she stumbles over a root. She lands hard on the forest floor, pine needles and dead leaves digging into her palms. She tries to move her legs, to get back up off of her elbows and fails. Her body screams to be still, to rest, to accept. Tears come as she lays her cheek on the ground. But the voices have followed her and they're so close and the earth is so comfortable. She closes her eyes. Allows her body to go lax. Perhaps she should just fall asleep and maybe they'll kill her quickly while she's unconscious. Easy and painless.

In the split second she falls into semi-consciousness, there is a familiar voice. Except it is sharp and desperate and right at her ear as it demands, "NO."

She jerks awake again and the voices are almost there, but there is something warm beneath her palm. Comforting. She lifts her palm and her breath catches. It's a seed.

The same seed from her dream.

Her cheek still pressed to the earth, she scratches into the dirt with one hand to make a hole. She nudges the seed into it then brushes soil to blanket it, soft, like she's stroking hair out of someone's eyes.

The voices are nearly deafening now. She has mere seconds before they reach her. She inhales deeply, hand over her seed's little bed, and exhales just as slowly. Warmth spreads in her chest like she's had a few swigs of rum, and it spreads down her arm and into the tips of her fingers where it tingles slightly.

"There she is!" - The voice of a guard. Likely Antonio. Antonio already didn't like her, and now she's gone and stabbed the prince. It sounds like dozens of men behind him. The light of their torches dances against her closed eyelids.

She clenches her hand into a hard fist and beside her - the earth erupts.

CHAPTER 3

There is a ringing in her ears, and her vision is blurry. She suddenly realizes she's a few yards away from where she used to be.

Where she used to be, there is something huge. It's some sort of cart - no - a chariot. Golden and ornate and impossible. Four horses stand in front of it, pitch black and about two times the size of the horses in her village. As she puzzles over the scene in front of her, black blocks her vision. She is leaning back on her elbows, teeth chattering and limbs shaking, and doesn't want to see what fresh hell she has brought upon herself so she just stares into the blackness. Then the blackness shifts and there is a person crouched in front of her but she keeps her gaze on the black, which she now understands is this person's clothes.

"Are you hurt?" the voice is low and deep with a slight growl beneath it. Familiar. A large hand cups her cheek, lifting her face. She's seen her before, she's almost certain. But she's also certain she would have remembered perfectly had she ever seen her before because she's just so intriguing. Her eyes are piercing and dark underneath black eyebrows, one of them cocked. Her nose is long and slightly crooked as if having been broken once. Her lips are pink and plump - lips no woman has any business having. Moles dot along her cheek, over her eyebrow, and one beneath her lower lip. She is beautiful, and Persephone can't seem to look away from her face. It draws her in. An intrinsic part of her body whispers to her to touch this person, to trace the marks on her face with her fingers. "Are. You. Hurt."

For fear of angering her, Persephone shakes her head though she doesn't know if she's hurt or not. Adrenaline rushes through her body, distracting her from any pain she may feel. It's hard for her to meet the stranger's eyes, her gaze is so sharp. Though the adrenaline makes her feel as light as a feather, the stranger's gaze tethers her to the earth, keeping her from floating away.

The woman rises to her full height and walks to where the prince's men are scattered, black cloak trailing behind her. The men are cowering in fear, some of them still on the ground. They curse in whispers, one weeps.

She speaks in a low voice, but she's too far away for Persephone to hear. Then the men start begging her, the highest-ranking among them on their knees in supplication. They have families, they cry.

"She has committed the highest treason," Antonio says. "She made an attempt on our regent's life! She is nothing more than a filthy whore and a traitor, my lord. We seek justice, that is all."

The woman in black glances back at her for a second. Persephone slowly gets to her feet when the woman turns her attention away, the adrenaline wearing off. Her legs ache. She doesn't trust this person not to side with them, and if she is on their side Persephone will receive much worse than any punishment the mortal men could mete out. She is powerful and tall and by the looks and sound of it, someone of considerable rank in the godly sphere. Not that Persephone would know who. Her mother never wanted her to be in contact with any other deities and therefore never allowed talk of them in their house. Too much danger, Demeter would say. And too much drama. Persephone had heard bits and pieces of the legends growing up in the village, but nothing substantial to give her any idea of who this woman is. She starts walking backward, trying to blend in with the forest and keep quiet. Each step hurts.

"Justice?" the stranger says. "Is thirty men against one woman justice?"

Antonio pales, shrinks back.

"It was a very serious crime, my lady. She was to be his bride."

The woman in black stiffens. There it is, Persephone thinks. She'll drag her back into the hands of the townsmen.

"I see," she says. She turns around to Persephone. "Come here."

The timbre of her voice nearly lulls Persephone into obedience, but not quite.

"I will not," she replies, cursing herself for the slight tremble in her words. She waits for the stranger to yell at her, but she remains expressionless, eyes cold.

"Tell your prince to choose a willing bride or none at all," the stranger says to the men. "You will leave now. And you will leave this woman alone."

She starts walking towards Persephone, when Antonio protests, "She is a traitor to the crown."

The woman in black whips around and is in Antonio's face in less than a second. She speaks almost in a growl. Persephone can't hear her words but Antonio backs away, face aghast, and then breaks into a run back towards the village. The head of the royal guard, running away in front of his men with his tail tucked between his legs. They quickly follow along. Their footsteps get further and further away, the woman in black not turning until they're inaudible.

Persephone can't help but collapse against the tree,

sliding down to sit at its base with her head in her hands. In relief and disbelief, and exhaustion. She can sense the woman in black getting near but she doesn't look up.

"Did you really try to kill a prince?" the stranger asks. She has crouched in front of Persephone again, and even crouched she seems tall.

"Yes."

The woman hums noncommittally.

"What did you say to them?" Persephone dares to ask.

"None of your concern."

"Who are you?"

At this the woman cocks her head, brow furrowed. She looks as if he's searching every inch of Persephone's face - for deceit?

"You don't know who I am."

"No. That's why I asked." Persephone is getting tired of this. The corner of the woman's mouth twitches up, but only for a second.

"Hades. God of the underworld. A pleasure to finally meet you."

That was interesting. The only information she'd gleaned about the god of the underworld was simply that - he was the god of the underworld. But she thought the god of the underworld was a man, and though she doesn't like to judge, this person does not carry themself as such. And something about the stranger's words was not right.

"Forgive me, but I thought the god of the underworld was a man. And what do you mean 'finally'?"

"Sometimes I'm a man. Not at the current epoch, though. It doesn't seem like you will be welcomed back to your village. Where will you go?"

Persephone's head spins. But she tries to focus on one thing at a time. She shrugs, "I don't know. But don't worry about it. I can take care of myself."

"I've no doubt about that."

"Thank you for helping me," she says, rising to her feet once more despite the deep ache. "You can go on about your night now. It was nice to meet you."

Hades stands up, catching Persephone's wrist before she can walk away. If a man touched her like this Persephone would rip out of his grasp like his flesh is made of hot coals. But Hades' hand is cool to the touch and gentle around her wrist as if she believes Persephone is made of paper. And it's oddly soothing, her voice and her touch.

"You can barely walk, Persephone," actual concern tints her voice. "Let me help you."

"You've done more than enough. Thank you, truly. I don't want to bother you any further."

Persephone makes to move away again and Hades' grip falls from her wrist to her hand.

"Make a deal with me," Hades says. "Your gift has not come in yet, has it?"

That stops her short. "How do you know that?"

"I can help you. Come with me, and I'll teach you."

"Come with you where?"

"My home. For only as long as it takes for you to get control over your gift. I know you are afraid. I won't hurt you."

"What's in it for you?"

She is quiet for so long that Persephone is about to repeat her question when Hades says, "Believe it or not, hell can get lonely."

That shocks her into silence. She had never considered it. For this warrior of a woman, with so much power that she rules the afterlife and judges souls, to be lonely.

"You want me to keep you company? And do what, play card games with you?"

"If you like card games."

Persephone groans and covers her face with a hand. What had she even been planning to do when she ran away from the house? She can't very well hide in the woods until her mother comes home. She loves nature and nature loves her, but she doesn't have the survival skills to last that long. She would if she had her gift. This woman, Hades, wants to help her. Give her a place to stay for practically nothing in return. Help her coax out her magic, and gods, how she has wanted that for so long.

"Okay, I'll try it. If I don't like it, you have to let me leave."

"Deal." Hades has the beginnings of a smirk on her face when she says, "You won't make attempted regicide a habit, will you? I'd be awfully put out if you tried to kill me."

"As long as you keep your word. If not, you'll end up like the last person that thought he could cross me," she is shaking as she says this, without knowing where the courage to do so came from.

Hades nods, solemn. "Whatever happened to you up here - it won't happen in my kingdom. No one will force you to do anything. On the off chance anyone tries, I should certainly hope you would leave them like you left the last man, or tell me and I'll do it for you."

By the severity of her gaze, Persephone knows she's genuine. "Okay," she says.

"Are you ready?"

"I suppose."

Hades gives a short whistle and her horses walk to them, chariot following behind. Though the chariot is huge and ornate, it will be a tight fit for two people. And it's obviously made for the 6'0 woman beside her, as the step up into it is high.

She holds out her hand for Persephone to take and helps her into the chariot, then steps in behind her, an arm on either side of her holding the reins. "Hold on," she says.

"To what?" Persephone asks. Before Hades can answer, the earth rumbles and opens up again, a gaping mouth ready to swallow them whole. She flicks the reins and they are moving so fast everything becomes a blur. Persephone grabs fistfuls of Hades' tunic and hides her face in its collar, heart in her throat.

She can feel the wind whipping around them and then the darkness - she can feel its coolness on her skin. She is not sure how long it takes them to fully descend into Hades' realm, but when she feels the chariot reach the ground her hands are aching from her tight grip on Hades' shirt, and her legs tremble.

"We're here," Hades says. Persephone doesn't open her eyes. There is such a stillness wherever they are. She can't hear birds chirping or insects clicking. She feels enclosed. She feels entombed. "Persephone."

She just shakes her head, not yet ready to face whatever she's gotten herself into, and still woozy from the flight. As if Hades can read her mind, she feels one of her arms wrap around her back and the other scoop up her knees so that she can carry her. And though she should not be letting this person she just met carry her - goddess or not, Persephone is not light and must be a strain - she knows not what else to do. She's so woozy and scared that she accepts this stranger's arms around her. Be it the exhaustion or shock, she falls unconscious to the swaying movements of her stranger's stride and the warmth of her embrace

CHAPTER 4

She is pinned down, and there is a sensation as if someone is trying to dig into her body, sharp pain that makes her jolt and cry out. The culprit suddenly materializes above her. Aetius. Teeth bared, eyes red from rum, blood spilling out of the wound in his shoulder. It pours down all over his shirt, his arms, and his hands. His hands also have her blood on them, like the first time he cornered her in the alleyway and broke into her. His breath is sour on her face. She can't move. She wants to rake her nails over his face, kick him in the ribs, scratch out his eyes, but some invisible force holds her down. She screams instead, and screams and screams and screams and something is grabbing her shoulder -

And she wakes up. She barely has time to take in her surroundings before she leans over the side of the bed and empties the contents of her stomach. Then she presses her face into the bedcover to muffle her groan. She has had nightmares about Aetius plenty of times, but this one is different. More visceral. More damaging. She feels disgusted and disgusting. She feels like dying.

"Persephone," comes a voice not too far away, quietly, gently. Hades.

Persephone doesn't have the energy to respond at first, but then she sits up with her back to Hades, remembering who, exactly, is in the room with her. She doesn't want to acknowledge what Hades just witnessed, doesn't want her to see her face.

"Where am I?" Persephone's voice is hoarse but steady.

"Your quarters. My realm. You are safe." Her voice is so assured. Calm and deep, like the forest at dusk.

"May I have a moment of privacy?"

"Of course, I'll have my housekeeper clean-"

"Please leave," her heart skips a beat, unsure how Hades will react to her rudeness. She knows she must look like a coastal town after a hurricane and there is literal vomit on the floor. And she still wants to peel her skin off after the dream. She is pushing it away now, but she knows she will feel humiliated later, at being seen like this. She wants to cry but there is so much empty in her that she finds she can't.

Hades sets something gently on the bed behind her and closes the door quietly behind her. When her footsteps have faded away outside, Persephone turns around to find a cool, damp cloth neatly folded. She wastes no time wiping her face, then she hops over the pool of sick and into the attached washroom. It's spacious, with a huge claw-foot tub that she begins to fill with water. The walls seem to be made out of slate, as if this room was carved out of a huge rock. The floor is black marble. There are curtains on the far side and she pushes them aside just a bit, to see a starry black sky and the shape of mountains on the horizon but she can't make out much else.

There are three knocks on her bedroom door then, and she is shocked to find a beautiful woman, tall with short blonde hair. She looks to be maybe forty in human years, although Persephone is unsure whether or not she is human. The woman has a kind smile and blue eyes that seem to know everything about Persephone already.

"Hello. I'm Sofia. I hear you're sick?"

She says it with so much kindness that Persephone begins to feel shy.

"Are you the housekeeper?" she asks Sofia.

"I am, indeed. May I come in?"

Persephone moves aside to let Sofia in and apologizes for the mess, which Sofia waves away.

"If I had some supplies I could clean it up myself," Persephone offers, feeling guilty.

"No, doll. I've got it."

"But-"

"I've got it," Sofia says, her face and voice firm, but gentle.

Sofia seems to be sizing up the mess, hands on her hips, before telling Persephone to go ahead and get a bath while she cleans. Persephone obeys. Despite how luxurious and fancy the tub is, it isn't hard to work. She strips and sighs as she sinks down into the warm water. She tries not to think too hard about the dream. She's survived this far in life focusing on the immediate moment before her, taking them one at a time. That's how she'll continue surviving.

When she is clean, she comes out of the bathroom to find two outfits on the bed, a simple dress, soft pink, and beside it a pair of brown trousers and a white shirt. How odd, she thinks to herself. Is it a test? In her kingdom, it is frowned upon for women to wear anything but dresses, though she knows in other parts of the world it is not so. It must not me so here, since Hades wore trousers yesterday. On some festival nights back home, Persephone could get away with wearing trousers if she put her hair up in a cap, but those nights were few and far between. She and her friend Lila would swagger around the festivities, pretending to be young bachelors and drinking their fill of mead. She misses Lila. She feels a sharp pain at the reminder and reaches for the dress. It's her favorite color.

And it isn't out of the ordinary, she could stay under the radar and make it out alive.

But then something stops her in her tracks. Her mother didn't raise her to be palatable.

If she is to survive down here perhaps she will have to be bold, show her toughness, radiate an aura of steel. She chooses the trousers. Hopes there will be no unforeseen consequences of it. She is not a fan of tests.

Unsure of what to do with herself after dressing, she glances out of the window once more. It is still night, it seems. She has no idea what time it is.

A rapping at her door interrupts her, so she turns away and opens the door despite the anxiety.

There Hades stands, in all black, tall and straight-backed.

"Are you feeling better?" she asks.

"Yes, thank you."

"And your quarters have everything you need?"

Persephone narrows her eyes. "What were you doing in here while I was sleeping?"

Hades' mouth sets in a firm line, but her eyes stay expressionless. "You were screaming."

"Oh," Persephone shifts. "Did I wake you?"

"No, but I thought you were being murdered."

Her first instinct is to apologize, but she catches herself before she does. No apologies here. No weakness.

"What time is it?"

"It's early in the morning. I would offer you breakfast but seeing as you just threw up-"

"How long will I be here again?"

"Until you get control of your power. Is it that bad?"

Persephone thinks about it. Her room is sleek and beautiful, with a black marble fireplace across from a big, cozy bed. She has her own washroom. She even has clothes that somehow are her exact size. Nothing has hurt her here yet.

"No," she admits. "It's perfect."

"Well, good. Would you like to see the rest?"

The rest of the sprawling castle is just as fiercely beautiful as her quarters. Long corridors with black marble floors and walls, sconces along the way flickering with blue flames. She wants to ask about it but gets distracted by the great mahogany doors of the dining room, which must be able to fit two hundred people. She imagines all the ghouls and demons of the underworld gathering here to dine and dance, and smiles to herself. But Hades' pace is brisk and shoulders set, so Persephone doesn't dawdle.

The kitchens are large and cozy, with a few normal, mortal-looking people kneading dough and washing pots. She smiles politely to them on their way through and they nod back at her. None of them bow to Hades, instead treating her like a passing peer. There are several bedrooms, lounges, and meeting rooms. There is a huge room which Hades informs her is their training area. Mirrors line the walls and a reed mat covers most of the floor. There is a rack on the other side of the room holding various weapons which she takes much interest in, but before she can touch one Hades tsks at her and leads her into the next room. Which happens to be the library.

It's breathtaking. Persephone asks Hades to let her stay a moment before continuing on the tour, and she obliges. She finds shelves upon shelves of books, and a nook with a marble fireplace like the one in her room, with a sofa and soft plush carpet in front of it. And like that, she's found her place in the castle.

Eventually, the tour ends with the throne room, where gods and minor deities and souls meet Hades. To socialize, discuss important matters, or to have their souls judged. This part of the castle feels much darker than the rest. The room is cavern-like, black stalactites pointing down from the ceiling like daggers waiting to fall. Stalactites merge and twine together to create the huge throne, spikes pointing from the top of the back. Upon each point is a skull. There are patterns etched into the seat and back, and along the arm rests. It's the most formidable thing she's ever seen.

"You are not to come in here while I'm working," Hades says, and Persephone lifts an eyebrow. Poor Hades, she thinks. If only she hadn't asked her not to, then she wouldn't have to do it.

"Understand?" Hades asks.

"I'm not a child. Don't talk to me like one."

Hades looks taken aback, which is satisfying but also terrifying. Persephone's not sure how far she can push yet. Hades' face turns cold.

"Did you forget who I am? That I saved your life?" she begins walking towards Persephone slowly.

"I didn't ask you to do that." Persephone's face is hot but she doesn't want to move away and show fear.

"On the contrary, you did." Hades is maybe a foot away from her now. Her answer surprises Persephone enough that her control slips and she backs up as Hades advances.

"How could I have?" Her back hits a wall. It's cool along her spine, helping ground her.

Hades shifts, pulling something from her pocket and holding it out to Persephone in her gloved hand. "Recognize this?"

It's a seed. The same little pod from her dream in the meadow, the one she planted in the soil next to her, exhausted, death heading her way in the form of forty mortal men. It had been pure instinct. Something inside of her knew the seed would lead to her salvation, but why was it Hades?

"How?" she asks.

"I don't know. But I heard you and you needed help, so I helped you. Remember, you don't have to be here if you don't want to be. I'll take you back right now," Hades says, shoving the seed into her hand.

"I never said I wanted to go back! Just that I won't be spoken to like a child. Are you that entitled that you would break our deal because I demand more respect?"

She watches Hades watch her, her own face red and fists clenched at her sides.

Hades is quiet for a few long moments. Persephone doesn't flinch. The reason she's down there in the first place is because of men who saw her as lesser than them. Though Hades is a goddess, more powerful than Persephone could ever hope to be, she is so tired of condescension.

Hades finally takes a step back out of her space.

"Please do not come in here when I'm working," she says.

"Okay," Persephone exhales a breath she didn't realize she was holding. "I won't, but can I ask why?"

"It's boring and you'll have better things to do."

Persephone can sense an omission of truth but lets it slide, for now. She's hungry. She'll find out what happens in the throne room later.

"When is lunch?" She asks.

Hades leads her back down into the kitchen where the cooks have prepared freshly baked bread, bowls of fruit, and some kind of delicious red soup. She sits at the counter in the kitchen instead of the grand dining room, at her request. Hades soon has to leave to attend to some underworldly duties, with the promise of dinner with her later. She eats and eats and eats until she feels fuller than she ever has. Then she is sated, warm, and drowsy, and one of the cooks shows her back to her room. She crawls back under the soft covers of her bed and falls into a comfortable sleep.

CHAPTER 5

Persephone eats at the proper dining table for dinner. Hades at the head of the table and Persephone immediately on her left. To Persephone's surprise, the rest of the table is filled with castle employees. She recognizes Sofia sitting next to a dark-haired woman. There are the kitchen workers she had seen on the tour, and countless other faces she didn't yet know. Before dinner officially begins, Hades stands at the head of the table and the room goes silent.

"Some of you have already met Persephone, but for those that haven't this is her," she gestures to Persephone's seated form. She stares at her plate as she feels the entire room's eyes on her, cheeks burning. "She will be staying with us for a while. Make her feel at home, please. And don't provoke her. She bites."

With that, Hades sits back down and everyone except Persephone begins doling servings onto their plates.

"You have such a way with words," Persephone mutters to her.

"Thank you. Will you pass the wine?"

Persephone grits her teeth and fills her cup before shoving the bottle at Hades. Despite her aggravation, she is delighted by the spread before them. Fresh-baked buttered rolls, roasted chicken, steamed greens, pasta in white sauce, and some kind of gravy fill the table with a heavenly aroma. She keeps to herself during dinner mostly, except to ask her neighbor on her left, a dryad with green freckles, to pass down more rolls. Hades is quiet too. Persephone gets the sense that she is monitoring her, but isn't sure for what. Signs of plans to escape? Murder?

Only once does Hades ask, "Are the rolls your favorite, then?"

With a mouthful of her fourth roll of the evening, she nods. After that, she wonders if maybe Hades is just looking at her to make sure she is enjoying the food. And she is, very much so.

After her second glass of wine, Persephone feels a little buoyant and she asks, "So when does training start?"

"Tomorrow morning. There should be some suitable clothes in your closet," Hades doesn't look up from cutting up the meat on her plate.

"Suitable clothes? Will I be physically exerting myself?"

"Of course."

"Oh."

Hades meets her eyes. "What did you think we would be doing?"

"I don't know. I just thought magic training was just like," she raises her closed fist and unfurls it quickly, popping her fingers out like she's seen her mother do when releasing a blast of magic.

The corner of Hades' lip quirks like she's about to smile, and informs her that wielding power is way more than hand gestures.

"It comes from your bones. Deep, deep inside. You'll see."

Persephone nods and her knee begins bouncing. She had somehow grown that flower in the forest. Will it feel like that again?

Before she can ask, a young man approaches Hades.

He's older than Persephone, but not by much. The points of his ears indicate fae heritage, or maybe nymph.

He nods to Hades in deference before Hades beckons him forward. The young man glances at Persephone and back to Hades, a pale sheen on his face.

"There is a matter I need to speak with you about, lord."

"Well obviously, Tari. What is it?"

"I rather hoped it could be a private conversation," the young man hedges.

"Anything you have to say can be said in front of her."

"The sun is rising."

Hades' face goes blank.

"But it's evening time," Persephone muses. She cranes her head to look at the large window at the end of the hall "It still looks dark to me out there?"

"Er, no ma'am. Things here are...different."

Hades has her gaze fixed straight ahead when she asks, "When did you know if this?"

"Villagers noticed something was off this morning, but it wasn't until fields in Asphodel began budding that we were sure."

Persephone can't help but notice the tenseness in Hades' posture, the way her hands grip the armrests of her chair.

Tari lowers his voice and says, "The council would like to speak with you, lord. After dinner."

"Of course," Hades nods, but her expression is distant. Tari bows and nods to Persephone then makes his leave.

After a moment, Persephone asks, "What's wrong with the sun rising?"

"It usually doesn't. The underworld has no sun."

Persephone thinks back to looking out her window. She had assumed it was late night or early morning because of the darkness. It's hard for her to fathom a life with no sun whatsoever.

"Is this...bad?" She doesn't want to be caught in any

more new and frightening situations. She would love for the underworld's affairs to be none of her business, but she figures they may affect her life now.

"I don't know. It's never happened." Hades takes another sip of wine and stands up. "I'll see you tomorrow morning in the training room."

She walks off, leaving Persephone alone at a table full of strangers.

It's the first time she's truly been out of her quarters without someone escorting her. Without Hades there to entertain or annoy her, she eats the rest of her meal in silence, stealing glances at other people at the table. They're all either talking animatedly with one another, or holding their spoon in one hand and a book in another, or just chewing in peace. They're content, she realizes. Totally at ease, even though they eat with the goddess of the underworld.

She is also certain that all the mortal kings and queens she's heard of would never, ever share a table with anyone non-royal. She's so strange, Persephone thinks. One minute Hades is intense and stone-faced, and the next she's earnest and gentle.

Persephone glances down the table at Sofia and a sudden pang hits her. Her mother. She has to contact her mother. She's a little ashamed that she hasn't thought of her sooner.

She finishes her dinner and sneaks a few rolls into her pocket for later. She turns to the person sitting next to her and politely asks, "Where should I put my plate?"

The person turns to her and she is taken aback by the rich, almost hypnotic brown of their eyes. Definitely not a mortal. "Please leave it, miss. We will take care of it."

"No, please. I don't want you to clean up after me."

"You are a friend of the Queen's. Such actions are beneath you," they give her a reassuring smile.

"Oh," her cheeks go pink. "Thank you but I'll just put it in the kitchen."

"Please let us do it, miss." they put their hand over one of hers, on the table. "Any guest of the Queen is a guest of ours too."

"What is your name?" Persephone asks.

"Trevan."

"Once again, thank you Trevan, really. I just prefer to do it myself," she smiles politely and gathers her dishes, sees Hades has left hers on the table and grabs them as well. She can feel eyes on her as she walks across the dining hall and into the huge kitchen. She washes the dishes in the basin, muttering to herself about spoiled, beautiful Queens.

Finding her bedroom again is only moderately difficult, mainly hindered by her curiosity about every door she comes across, every divine statue, every broad window. Eventually, she does find her door and rifles through the desk that sits in front of her window. She gets to work with parchment and quill on a letter to her mother, scratching out and rewriting every other sentence.

Hi Mama,

I hope this letter finds you well. As you may or may not have heard by now, I stabbed the prince. I had a good reason, though. A reason that I prefer to tell you when I see you again. I almost died, but the god of the underworld saved me. The other kids always said Hades was a man, but she's a woman "at this current epoch" (her words exactly). She says she can help me with my power. So as of now, I am in hiding - of sorts- at her castle. Don't know how I feel about her yet. It would have been easier if you had taught me anything about the other deities, but I'm having to find out for myself. This is a lot at once, I'm sorry. I am safe. I'll come home when I can.

Love you very much,

Persephone.

It's not perfect, but it's the best she can do at the moment. The next time she sees Sofia, she'll ask about sending it off.

Training is hell. But she *is* in hell, isn't she? She arrives at the training room in leggings and a loose shirt, nervous but raring to go. She nearly stops short at the sight of Hades in a sleeveless, tight, black shirt and pants. She is twirling a staff in one hand and Persephone's heart jumps. Will she get to spar with her?

"Good morning," Hades says, looking her up and down. "Take your shoes off."

Persephone does without question, as Hades also is barefoot. The floor is cool beneath her soles.

"We are going to start with meditation. Sit across from me," Hades says.

Persephone frowns but does as she's told. Meditation to her seems like a whole lot of doing nothing. But Hades bids her close her eyes and fill her lungs as full as she can, pushing all thoughts out of her mind. Persephone does it somewhat sarcastically, finding it impossible to think of nothing. Especially with Hades sitting across from her, strong and lovely and close enough to smell the pine of her cologne. Or do gods have to wear cologne? Can they use magic to make themselves smell alluring?

"Persephone," she breaks the silence. "You're not concentrating."

"I'm trying! It's hard and I don't see how it will help me learn."

"You have to center yourself before you can learn. Feel yourself in your body, your body as an extension of yourself. Try again."

They sit in silence for another five minutes and Persephone is on the verge of dozing off when Hades stands abruptly.

"This isn't working," she says, and it's too accusatory for Persephone's liking.

"It's not my fault."

"Yes, it is." She steps back and stares intently into Persephone's eyes as if searching. "You don't want to feel yourself in your body, do you?"

"Not really I suppose?"

"Why?"

"I don't know. Can't we spar or something?"

"No." Hades steps closer and slowly extends a hand to her.

"What is this?" Persephone asks, gesturing between Hades' hand and her.

"Just take it," she snarls.

Persephone finally does and tamps down her delight at how Hades' hands are slightly bigger than her own, and how warm the black leather of her glove is against her palm.

"Sit with me again."

They sit across from each other, just like before, only linked this time.

"Now," Hades says, picking up Persephone's other hand too. Their faces are only a foot away, and Persephone notices that her eyes are deep, deep brown. The kind that would turn amber in the sunlight. "Close your eyes."

She does. Hades instructs her just as before, to breathe deeply. It's easier this time. The pressure of her hold on Persephone's hands, and her mere proximity, make it difficult to focus on anything else. They sit with only the sounds of their breathing. Something settles inside of Persephone and it feels clean. Calm. She finds the dark behind her eyelids comforting. She could stay that way, in perfect stillness, in the warmth of their touch, forever. And in that calm, there is a well. She can almost see it. Deep and quiet. Waiting.

She only notices that Hades let go of one of her hands

when her glove touches her face. Persephone opens her eyes slowly as Hades smooths her thumb over her cheek, perfectly at peace with being touched like this. She feels a little new, or maybe ancient instead. And the way Hades is looking at her is also a discovery, sort of like the way she watches double rainbows arch over the meadow on rare summer afternoons.

"It worked," Persephone says.

The corner of Hades' mouth crooks up, and she replies, "I can tell."

CHAPTER 6

Demeter had only once before had this feeling. This sense of foreboding blanketing the very ground she walks. The rocks beneath her soles seem sharper, the grass itchier.

The first time was after she first learned she was pregnant. She had been overjoyed despite the father's indifference. To him, it was the consequence of a quick dalliance while Hera was away. To her, it was a sign she would never be alone again. She hadn't cared for Zeus, no. He was, however, very seductive and told her Hera was away with her own lover. Demeter would never have done it had she known the truth; that Hera was only visiting Hestia. But Demeter could never bring herself to regret the accidental betrayal of Hera. It gave her the blessing of Persephone.

She visited the oracle while pregnant, eager to learn about the child in her belly.

She wanted to know what powers the baby might have, what great things they might do. Instead, she was told of a grave fate.

Her child would grow up to be stolen by another god. Demeter was suspicious it might be Zeus, but he had never shown much interest in his children. Why would that change with Persephone? She pressed the oracle for more information, but the only other thing it would say is that there would be a great divide. The destruction of the kingdom of the gods, all the fault of her child.

Demeter left the oracle and fled Olympus in the dead of night. The further she fled, the more the weight lifted from her chest. She would keep her child far, far away from the celestial kingdom. She would ensure no one ever found them.

Now, she's running out to the stables to get her horse. There's that same feeling she had twenty-one years ago when she was told her baby would be taken. It's a pit in her stomach. A boulder in her heart. Something is wrong, and it involves Persephone.

CHAPTER 7

If there's one thing Persephone knows how to do, it's wait. Waiting to have power. Waiting for her mother to come home. Waiting for Aetius to leave her be.

And now she's waiting for something. Anything. She hasn't seen Hades since dinner. She sits on her bed, kicking her legs back and forth. Wondering what is to come next.

Perhaps she could go to the library? She assumes she is allowed since Hades showed it to her in the first place. But then again, passing my time in the underworld by reading a book feels wasteful. She should be out somewhere, honing her skills. If she were at home she would have various chores around the house to keep her busy, but she has no cleaning supplies on hand and everything in her quarters is already clean. Or occasionally, she would pass the time by baking. Most of the time she was in the wild. She's not sure what kind of wild is outside of her window, here. Better not risk it.

She opens her door to find Hades standing outside, fist raised as if about to knock.

"Hello," Persephone says.

"Where are you off to?"

"I was going to the library. I assume that's alright?"

"Yes, of course."

"Did you need something?"

"I hope the dinner agreed with you."

"It was delicious. You should have taken your dishes to the kitchens."

Hades cocks her head.

"I have staff to do that for me."

"But why? Surely you can do it on your own?"

"Persephone," she starts. "I am the goddess of the underworld. I have responsibilities to attend to almost every minute I live and breathe. Forgive me if I don't take my dishes to the kitchens for cleaning."

"What kind of responsibilities?"

"Has your mother told you nothing?"

"What do you know of my mother?"

Upon seeing Persephone's blank expression she says, "Walk with me."

Persephone does. Side by side, they stroll through the hallways. She doesn't know where Hades is taking her or if she even knows.

"What, exactly, do you know of the gods?"

Persephone wrinkles her nose. "I know my mother is Demeter, goddess of the harvest. I know I am Persephone. I know my father was also a god, but not a very good one. I've heard bits and pieces from others in the village, but not much."

"Not much, huh?" Hades sounds angry, almost.

"My mother said that's all I needed to know. Gods are fickle, selfish beings and I'm glad to be separated from them, no offense."

"None taken. Your father is my brother."

"What?" Persephone rounds on Hades fast. Her voice comes out more like a squeak than a question.

"It's not like that. The celestial family is different. Family ties in the human world are too close," Hades fumbles into a brief silence, frustrated. "We are not made of the same material as them, Persephone. Every time a god is made they are made of completely new material, not material from their parents."

"Okay?"

"It's more like two beings coming together to fashion something out of clay. They work together, but the material is neither of theirs. Ultimately, it is the Earth's. Although, sometimes a god can make another all on their own. Your father-"

"Please stop referring to him as my father. He is nothing of the sort. Emotionally, or otherwise, apparently."

"Okay, so Zeus made Athena on his own. Quite a ridiculous story."

"Who's Athena?"

"Oh, dear. You have so much to learn."

"Are you my aunt?"

"No. Gods, no."

"But you're Zeus's sibling – Zeus who made me, with my mother?"

"By human standards, perhaps. But we are not human."

"Maybe I am. Maybe my mother and Zeus accidentally made me without whatever spark makes a goddess."

Hades turns to her, stopping them both in the middle of the corridor.

"Don't you ever say that." Her voice is deep, stony. "Ever. You are celestial, and you will come into your power."

"What if I never do?"

"Then you're still celestial. There's something about you that reeks of it."

This stranger believes in her so much. Persephone feels tears burning her eyes, but she tries to blink them away. She keeps her head down when she says, "Are you saying I smell?"

Hades has a big laugh, not an obnoxious one, but one

that fills the space with pure joy. Persephone can't help but giggle with her.

"On the contrary, you smell like lavender. Today. Yesterday, however…"

"I had been running for my life!"

"I'm joking. Even when you were sweaty and filthy, I could smell lavender under it all."

"Odd."

"Not really. You'll have to accept that you're extraordinary sometime, you know."

Persephone shrugs it off, too used to disappointment to dare to believe it. Instead she thinks about the fact that just laughed with the goddess of the underworld. It's a stark change from twenty-four hours before when she thought she would never live to see daylight again.

She discovers Hades is taking her outside. They arrive at two large wooden doors at the back of the castle. Hades snaps her fingers and they open wide.

Cool air brushes against Persephone's face and Hades steps out into the night.

"Coming?" she asks.

"Is it safe out there?"

"Mostly."

"You think you're funny."

"I like to think so, yes. But truthfully, you're with me and nothing will touch you when you're with me." There's a breeze floating in, toying with the flyaway hairs that didn't make it into Hades' bun.

"What's out there?" Persephone nearly whispers. Perhaps because she doesn't want whatever's out there to hear her fear.

"Plants. Animals. Trees. The like."

"I don't appreciate your sarcasm. I'm serious."

Hades steps back through the doorway, holds her hand out to her. "I promise you're safe."

Her voice has that low timbre that has come to reassure her a few times, she is being genuine.

Persephone slips her hand in Hades'. She doesn't notice how cold her own hands are until their skin touches. Hades is not wearing gloves. Their fingers do not intertwine. Instead, Hades' press against the back of Persephone's hand, their palms together. The goddess's skin is so warm on hers. She is walking Persephone outside, but all Persephone can think about is her callouses. And what sort of physical labor the queen of the underworld must do. Aetius never had any callouses, or scars, or anything about him that would suggest hardship. Perhaps he'll have one now that she's stabbed him.

Hades is pulling her gently behind her, and speaking in earnest of the garden around them. Underfoot is cobblestone, with marble dotting the landscape here and there in the form of statues or fountains or plant pots. Persephone does not recognize any of the plant life. Much of it is prickly, thorned stems and black or red petals. Similar to roses, perhaps, but the petals look veiny and shimmery and not quite as petals should.

"What do you call these?" she asks, realizing a second too late that she interrupted Hades.

"Night Blossoms."

"Beautiful name."

"Do you like them?"

"They are...odd. May I touch them?"

"Of course." Hades lets her hand go, presumably to allow her closer to the plants, but Persephone grabs it back and pulls her along. She doesn't totally feel safe yet. She feels like there could be things in the bushes or crouching in branches and she will not let Hades go even for a second. She thanks the heavens Hades doesn't say anything about it.

Persephone trails her index finger along one of the petals and the plant *reacts*. It seems to shiver, almost. Whatever shimmery dust it gives off coats her fingers. When she pulls her hand away the plant leans towards it and she nearly shrieks.

"Do they all do that?" she demands, breathless. She has jumped two feet back from the thing, straight into Hades' chest. Her breath brushes the top of Persephone's head, a hand resting gently at her waist. It's embarrassing. It feels good. Persephone doesn't look away from the plant.

"They don't, actually," Hades says. Something in her voice tilts and Persephone gets the feeling she's as caught off-guard as she is. That's worrying.

Persephone steps away from her. "Did I mess it up or something?"

"I don't believe so. Will you try it again?"

"It's not going to attack me, is it?"

"I doubt it."

"Oh, gods." Even so, she creeps back towards it. This time, she touches the blossom right beside it. The same thing happens. The stem shivers, it leans into her.

"This has never happened before. Back home. What is this?"

"I don't know, Persephone. I think they just like you," Hades laughs.

Persephone is not sure why, but as they walk the rest of the trail through the greenery, she trails her palm against each plant. They all pull towards her, even as she walks away. She'll look behind her and it's as if a thousand little faces are watching her go. Not all of them have that same shimmery dust on them. There are huge trees, some too tall to climb, others the perfect height. Some bear strange fruit with bright colors, oranges, greens, blues, yellows, some streaked, some dotted. There is one tree nearly hidden behind the others, back away from the pathway. There's a small clearing surrounding it. Little bugs glow around it, bouncing here and there. They remind her of the fireflies from home, but these do not blink in and out. And they are a multitude of colors. The tree in the middle has branches that hang, laden with round fruit of a dark red hue, so deep they're almost purple.

"Can we go in there?" she asks her tour guide.

After a second or two in which she thinks Hades may deny her, she nods. Once Persephone's feet are off the hard stone and onto natural ground, she takes shoes off and leaves them on the path. The grass is cool and soft against her soles and she'd like to dance upon it, to have foot meet earth over and over because gods, it feels like a breath of fresh air. She is not built to be inside all day.

She lets go of Hades to try and cup one of the glowing insects in her palms. They float here and there, never letting her catch them. She gives up and approaches the tree. It's pretty large and its branches spread overhead. She could reach up right now and pluck down a fruit. She lifts an arm to do just that. Her fingers barely brush its purpled skin when Hades grabs her wrist. Not hard, but enough to be a warning. Enough to startle her.

"What?"

"Don't eat from this tree. It's poisonous."

"You could have just told me that." She slips her wrist free of her grasp, annoyed. That Hades can frighten her, does frighten her, makes her feel safe just for her to jump out of her skin the next minute.

"I would like to go back inside now," Persephone says, unable to look at her. It's an overreaction, she knows, but she also knows no other way to respond to fear.

"I'm sorry, Persephone."

The sorrow with which Hades says it makes her eyes prickle and she knows tears will come soon if she doesn't leave immediately, so she turns back. She hates being this fretful, restless thing, always on a knife's edge. All Hades did was grab her wrist.

She follows Persephone closely. "Did I hurt you?"

Persephone shakes her head and slips her shoes back on.

"I didn't mean to startle you. Please don't go."

"I'm just going back to my room. It's fine. It's nothing. I'm tired."

"It's not fine. You're crying."

"So?" Persephone wipes the tears from her cheeks, glaring at a bush across the path. It's hard enough to be crying in front of Hades and to have her know she is crying, that Persephone can't look into her eyes and be here like this at the same time. There's too much shame.

"I'll be more careful from now on. I won't grab you like that again, I just didn't want you to poison yourself. There's so much more out here that I know you'll love to see."

"How do you know?" she mumbles.

"There's a tree near the back wall that sings."

She whips her head up at that. "No way."

"Come on." Hades walks backward slowly, toward the thicker foliage deeper in the garden. She's playful, almost. Persephone follows.

About an hour later, both tired and hyper, Persephone can't stop babbling about what she saw. They are walking through the corridors on the way back to her rooms. Hades listens, adding or exclaiming here and there.

"The tree didn't actually sing," Persephone argues. The tree in question had naturally formed holes along its branches and trunks that made low hums when the wind blew through them. It was miraculous, to her.

"How do you know? Just because it doesn't have a mouth as we do doesn't mean it can't sing."

"Singing implies vocal cords - Do you think I could have plants in my rooms?"

"I'd like to think the tree formed its equivalent of vocal cords - and absolutely, if you want them."

"Not a cut bouquet or anything. Do you have pots I could plant some in?"

"Of course. I'll ask Sofia."

"I don't want to trouble her. If you tell me where they are I can do it myself."

"She'll help you find them. I don't know where they are. It's been a while since there has been any planting inside the castle."

"Since when?"

"Since forever, maybe."

"You don't have any plants in your room?"

"No, I don't."

"You should. They're good for your mind."

They've now reached Persephone's door and she loathes to part with her companion. She hasn't talked to someone like this, free and open, someone that was not her mother, in so long. Maybe since her friend Lila left the village a few years back. She wanted badly to be friends with the other kids her age in the village but something always stopped her. It was like there was a thin film between her and the others and it made her hesitate before joining any games of hopscotch or marbles or the occasional secret poker game beneath the bakery's back steps. Most of the kids were nice enough to her, but her doubt and insecurities isolated her.

But now she is here, in the underworld, with one of the most powerful goddesses by her side listening to her ramble and prod and wonder. And she seems to enjoy it.

"We're training again tomorrow, right?"

"Yes. If you can get your meditations down maybe we could spend a little time on physical combat."

"Physical combat?" It comes out a bit too excitedly, so Persephone adds, "What does that have to do with anything?"

"It may take a while for you to get a handle on your power. In the meantime, wouldn't you like to be able to defend yourself?"

"You make it sound like things are coming after me left and right. I'm not some damsel."

"Absolutely not. I just meant maybe it would give you some peace of mind."

"I would rather just focus on bringing out the power, so I don't have to resort to my fists."

"Fair enough. The offer is always on the table,

though."
"Okay."
"Okay."
"Goodnight, Persephone."
"Goodnight."

Hades nods and heads down the hallway, to her rooms, Persephone assumes. As she gets ready for bed, she wonders about them. Are they as dark as Hades is? Her pants, tunics, boots, and cape are always pitch black. Her hair is pitch black. Her eyes, however, are warm brown, and very serious.

Persephone sinks in the warm water of her bath and sighs. Whatever tomorrow will bring, it will be exciting and exhausting, she's sure of it.

She dreams of Aetius and his grotesque hands on her and that feeling of being weighed down by tons and tons, and then Hades is there and Aetius is not. Hades is touching Persephone with her beautiful hands and the weight lightens from smothering to grounding, like she is loved. Like Hades is there, body covering hers, head on her chest. Then all at once, there is no weight, good or bad. Hades is sucked away from her and there stands her mother. She's distraught and frazzled and angry. Persephone wants to tell her it's all okay. She wants to hug her. But it feels like there is cotton filling up the space between them and her voice does not work and her limbs do not work. Her mother stares at her, in worry and something else she can't place.

"Persephone," she demands. "Where are you?"

And all Persephone can do is look back at her.

CHAPTER 8

Training the next morning is a little awkward. She can't stop thinking about the dream she had, or dreams, she isn't sure if it was one long dream or a series of short ones blending together. Hades is once again sitting across from her, holding her hands. She reaches that ball of light within her much quicker than she did yesterday. It tingles through her scalp and fingertips and toes, leaving goosebumps in its wake.

"Good, good." Hades croons. Persephone beams, eyes closed. "Now I'm going to let go. See if you can keep in contact with it."

She begins to pull her hands away from Persephone's, slowly. Persephone imagines there is a thread between them, and as Hades pulls away she sees herself gripping the end of it and holding it to her chest. But no matter how hard she tries, she can't hold on to the thread, to the power.

"No!" she grabs Hades' hands before she lets go fully. "Don't. I can't stand the feeling, not having it."

"You'll have to, someday. All I am doing is being a conduit between you and the power. You need to create your own relationship with it."

Persephone opens her eyes to find Hades looking at her.

"How on earth do I do that?"

"Honestly, I'm not sure."

"How did you do it?"

"I never did."

Oh. She was born with her power. She didn't have to wait for it to come in, or work for it. It just happened for her.

Persephone slips her hands away. "What is wrong with me?"

"Nothing is wrong with you-"

"This isn't normal. Mother told me it was, that I'd just have to wait for it-"

"Persephone-"

"Did she lie to me?"

Hades looks hard at her. Persephone knows she's deliberating.

"Just tell me. Please."

"This is the first time I've heard of someone not having their power from birth. But I can feel it in you, it's there. We just have to bring it out."

Persephone can feel herself wanting to cry, again. But she looks away from Hades and does her best to compose herself. Her mother didn't tell her anything, she now realizes. Nothing about being celestial. Why?

"Hey," Hades says, tucking a lock of Persephone's hair behind her ear. She's too tender to be the ruthless god she's rumored to be. Persephone secretly revels in the brush of her fingertips over the curve of her ear. She pushes Persephone's jaw with one of her knuckles, demanding she looks at her once more. "You're magnificent."

A rush of warmth overcomes Persephone, and she knows her cheeks are turning red. But she can't think of how to respond and so she doesn't.

"Shall we try again?" Hades asks.

Persephone nods. This time, she imagines the light as the thread, attaching her to the earth. She pulls as hard as she can, and when Hades slips her hands out of hers she can still feel it buzzing in her palms, very small and flickering, but still there.

"You're doing it," Hades says. Persephone doesn't know how she knows. At the moment she can't bring herself to care. This is huge progress, even though the bit of light she holds onto is tiny. She opens her eyes. Hades is smiling at her. It's a novel thing, a few of her teeth are a bit crooked and her two canines are sharper than they should be, but there is pride in her eyes. She is proud of Persephone. Persephone is proud of herself. She looks down at her hands in her lap, turned palms-up and she can see it - physical light, power, the celestial. It tickles a bit. She lets out a breathless laugh, elation blooming in her chest. But it is tiring, holding on so tight to it, and she eventually has to let go. When the light in her hands dies down, she has to catch her breath. She notices Hades is properly staring at her.

"What?"

"Beside you."

She looks and finds a small flower has bloomed a few inches from her left knee. It's a tiny yellow daffodil, the kind she and her mother planted beneath the windows of their cottage when she was younger.

"Did I do that?"

Hades nods, lips curved up at the edge still.

"Oh," Persephone says quietly. "Oh, my gods!" She jumps to her feet and exclaims, "I did that!"

Hades follows her up. "Yes, you did. How shall we celebrate?"

"I don't even know!" She balls her hands into fists, not out of anger, but to prevent herself from clapping her hands excitedly like a child who's gotten a present on Yuletide.

"I think we'll have a ball in your honor."

"A ball? You have balls in the underworld?"

"Every once in a while."

"I've never been to one." Persephone's been invited every year. But the balls were hosted by the royal family and even before he attacked her that first time she knew to avoid him. Her mother gave her the choice of whether she wanted to go or not, and she always said no. But oh, how she wanted to dance.

"Is that so?"

Persephone nods.

"It'll be great. But first, you have to pick out what to wear."

CHAPTER 9

Training the next morning is a little awkward. She can't stop thinking about the dream she had, or dreams, she isn't sure if it was one long dream or a series of short ones blending together. Hades is once again sitting across from her, holding her hands. She reaches that ball of light within her much quicker than she did yesterday. It tingles through her scalp and fingertips and toes, leaving goosebumps in its wake.

"Good, good." Hades croons. Persephone beams, eyes closed. "Now I'm going to let go. See if you can keep in contact with it."

She begins to pull her hands away from Persephone's, slowly. Persephone imagines there is a thread between them, and as Hades pulls away she sees herself gripping the end of it and holding it to her chest. But no matter how hard she tries, she can't hold on to the thread, to the power.

"No!" she grabs Hades' hands before she lets go fully. "Don't. I can't stand the feeling, not having it."

"You'll have to, someday. All I am doing is being a conduit between you and the power. You need to create your own relationship with it."

Persephone opens her eyes to find Hades looking at her.

"How on earth do I do that?"

"Honestly, I'm not sure."

"How did you do it?"

"I never did."

Oh. She was born with her power. She didn't have to wait for it to come in, or work for it. It just happened for her.

Persephone slips her hands away. "What is wrong with me?"

"Nothing is wrong with you-"

"This isn't normal. Mother told me it was, that I'd just have to wait for it-"

"Persephone-"

"Did she lie to me?"

Hades looks hard at her. Persephone knows she's deliberating.

"Just tell me. Please."

"This is the first time I've heard of someone not having their power from birth. But I can feel it in you, it's there. We just have to bring it out."

Persephone can feel herself wanting to cry, again. But she looks away from Hades and does her best to compose herself. Her mother didn't tell her anything, she now realizes. Nothing about being celestial. Why?

"Hey," Hades says, tucking a lock of Persephone's hair behind her ear. She's too tender to be the ruthless god she's rumored to be. Persephone secretly revels in the brush of her fingertips over the curve of her ear. She pushes Persephone's jaw with one of her knuckles, demanding she looks at her once more. "You're magnificent."

A rush of warmth overcomes Persephone, and she knows her cheeks are turning red. But she can't think of how to respond and so she doesn't.

"Shall we try again?" Hades asks.

Persephone nods. This time, she imagines the light as the thread, attaching her to the earth. She pulls as hard as she can, and when Hades slips her hands out of hers she can still feel it buzzing in her palms, very small and flickering, but still there.

"You're doing it," Hades says. Persephone doesn't know how she knows. At the moment she can't bring herself to care. This is huge progress, even though the bit of light she holds onto is tiny. She opens her eyes. Hades is smiling at her. It's a novel thing, a few of her teeth are a bit crooked and her two canines are sharper than they should be, but there is pride in her eyes. She is proud of Persephone. Persephone is proud of herself. She looks down at her hands in her lap, turned palms-up and she can see it - physical light, power, the celestial. It tickles a bit. She lets out a breathless laugh, elation blooming in her chest. But it is tiring, holding on so tight to it, and she eventually has to let go. When the light in her hands dies down, she has to catch her breath. She notices Hades is properly staring at her.

"What?"

"Beside you."

She looks and finds a small flower has bloomed a few inches from her left knee. It's a tiny yellow daffodil, the kind she and her mother planted beneath the windows of their cottage when she was younger.

"Did I do that?"

Hades nods, lips curved up at the edge still.

"Oh," Persephone says quietly. "Oh, my gods!" She jumps to her feet and exclaims, "I did that!"

Hades follows her up. "Yes, you did. How shall we celebrate?"

"I don't even know!" She balls her hands into fists, not out of anger, but to prevent herself from clapping her hands excitedly like a child who's gotten a present on Yuletide.

"I think we'll have a ball in your honor."

"A ball? You have balls in the underworld?"

"Every once in a while."

"I've never been to one." Persephone's been invited every year. But the balls were hosted by the royal family and even before he attacked her that first time she knew to avoid him. Her mother gave her the choice of whether she wanted to go or not, and she always said no. But oh, how she wanted to dance.

"Is that so?"

Persephone nods.

"It'll be great. But first, you have to pick out what to wear."

They walk outside the front entrance this time, grand and ornate and obsidian. They make their way down a well-worn pathway through a thicket of trees, towards a town that Hades says is not too far from the castle. Persephone hadn't given much thought to the underworld, but she certainly didn't think there would be towns. Civilizations. Others in the mortal realm had made it sound like a pit of dead suffering. The sky above is still dark, but not as pitch-black as it was when she first arrived here. She remembers what Tari said yesterday, about the sun rising.

"Has the sun actually risen yet?" she asks.

"Not fully. Just a bit each day. It's brighter today than it was yesterday, and brighter yesterday than it was the day before. I imagine eventually it will rise and fall as fully it does in the mortal realm."

"What will happen to the night blossoms? Won't they die?"

Hades lets out a gruff laugh. "That's what you're worried about?"

"Aren't you worried?"

"Not entirely."

"Why not? Didn't you say this has never happened

before?"

"Honestly?"

Persephone nods at her to go on.

"I think it's you."

They lapse into silence, Hades' one of waiting, Persephone's one of shock. But when she thinks about it really, it makes sense. And in some way, she knew it before. That's the only explanation. It began when she came here. But how could her presence cause such a shift? She has a tenuous, mostly non-existent relationship to her power. Could she really conjure up an entire sun?

Twigs and leaves crunch underfoot.

Just to refute Hades and fill the quiet she asks, "How can you be sure?"

"Being the queen of the underworld, I have a sort of… connection to it. I can feel it. If something was seriously wrong I would know it. But it doesn't feel like that. It feels warm. It just feels like you."

"You can feel…people?"

"Somewhat. You most of all."

"Can you read my mind?" Persephone demands, blush rising in her cheeks.

"No, it's not like that. I can feel an echo of what you feel, almost. And the signature of your magic, your presence."

"Is it normal to feel other people's emotions?"

"No."

She doesn't know what to say to that. She doesn't want to think about what that means for her. She looks intently at the branches of the trees, every once in a while spying small glowing eyes peering at her. Maybe they're little, scruffy creatures like the squirrels of the mortal realm. Maybe they're grotesque beasts that would gnaw the meat from her bones if Hades were not here.

The 'town' she mentioned before turns out to be a city. People and creatures of all kinds call out wares from the sides of the streets, under the awnings of buildings. They pass some sort of bakery with goods Persephone's never seen before but smell delicious. There's a bookstore with tomes of many colors and sizes, and some seem sentient, judging by how one of the satyr shopkeepers runs after a rogue title that has chosen to take flight. There are restaurants and blacksmiths and cobblers and all manner of businesses.

Her mother has only taken her to the big mortal city a day's travel away from their village a few times. It wasn't too different from this city, except that there are no beggars here. There is no one sitting in the alleyways in tattered clothing and haunted eyes. She makes a note to ask Hades about it later.

Speaking of Hades, Persephone expected fanfare and bowing in the city when the townspeople saw her. Instead, many of them give their queen a smile or a respectful nod. It is an entirely different world than home, she thinks.

She isn't sure what she imagined the underworld to be, but it isn't this. The people of the city are of all kinds, with an array of hooves, horns, wings, tails. Some of them she knows would be regarded as monsters in the mortal realm, but here they just exist beside their neighbors, no matter how sharp their teeth are.

Hades leads her to a small shop with a wooden sign hanging above it, the name "Kyrie's" painted in elegant curlicue.

"Kyrie is an excellent friend of mine," Hades says. She opens the door and a small tinkling sound announces their arrival. A highly-styled person steps out of a backroom, white-blonde locks in shocking contrast to their dark skin.

"Well if it isn't the devil herself," the person smiles warmly at Hades, and when their eyes land on Persephone, they light up even more. "And who is this?"

"This is my guest, Persephone. Persephone, this is Kyrie."

"You can call me Ky. Any friend of Hades is a friend of mine."

Persephone smiles at them, feeling a tad shy at this person's friendliness.

"We're looking for something nice," Hades says. "There's a ball tonight in her honor."

"How exciting!" Ky addresses Persephone, "What sort of something nice?"

Persephone shrugs. "I'm not certain. What do you have?"

"A lot. Am I invited to the ball?"

"I don't know," Hades replies. "The last time you and I drank together you ended up asleep on the castle roof."

Persephone lets out a surprised laugh, and Kyrie shakes their head. "Number one, you dared me to climb up there and number two, you're a worse drunk than I am. I'm inviting myself. Rude." Ky walks toward the back of the store, throwing over their shoulder, "Take a look around for a moment while I gather my things,"

Persephone takes in the little shop for the first time. There are shimmering gowns, and garments that look like gowns but upon closer inspection have pant legs. There are shining jackets and brocade breeches and corsets with so much beading one can't even see the fabric underneath.

"Everything is so beautiful," Persephone whispers. "Where are the prices? I don't have much money." She actually has no money at all, but she doesn't want Hades to know that.

"Don't worry about the price," Hades says. "I've got you."

Upon seeing worry furrowing Persephone's brow, she adds, "Things aren't too expensive here anyway. Everyone has what they need, and then some."

"That doesn't seem possible." Persephone shakes her head, moving on to the next display of fabrics, gossamer and silk and patterned and sheer.

Ky pops out again, carrying a measuring tape, pins, and all assortment of odds and ends.

"Back here, doll." They beckon Persephone to the rear of the shop, where a small pedestal stands and there are mirrors all around. "Stand right up here and I'll get your measurements."

She does, though uncomfortable with being the center of both Ky and Hades' attention. Ky is swift and chatty, not for a second letting her fall into awkward silence. They raise her arms at one point and measure her bust, her waist. Then they move on to her height, arm length, and even her neck length which she never imagined would matter in a garment fitting. "You have legs for days and days. And your hips!" Ky throws their hands in the air with the outburst.

That makes her blush profusely. Somewhere around the age of eleven, the tallest of the girls her age and chubby to boot, she learned to wish for petite features. She never loved bringing attention to her height, or her weight.

"It's a compliment," Hades amends.

"Oh," Persephone smiles weakly. "Thank you." She wonders how Hades got into the habit of reading her so well.

"Did anything catch your eye?" Ky asks, gesturing to the front of the store.

"Pretty much everything. I have no clue what I'm looking for."

"No worries. I'll bring a few for you to try and tell me what you think of them, alright?"

She nods. "May I get down now?"

At Ky's affirmative, Hades offers her hand to help Persephone step down, as if it's a difficult task to step 12 inches down. Persephone doesn't complain, however.

For the rest of their visit, Ky makes her try on outfit after outfit, helping her dress and undress behind the cover of a gilded screen. She learns very quickly that her insecurities do not matter around them. They pull fabrics over her hips and lace up the backs of dresses with the same efficiency as a seasoned baker would lay a pie crust or crack an egg. Or her mother snipping dead leaves and plucking ripe vegetables. Nearly every piece they put on her body she falls in love with. There is a pair of heavily embroidered breeches with a matching jacket that cinches at the waist, when she walks out to show to Hades she breaks into a grin, and Persephone does too. But ultimately, the inside itches at her skin and she forgoes them both. Many dresses accentuate her bust, her back, her hips, but there is always something not quite right about it. Maybe it's the way that her thighs rub together underneath the skirts that get on her nerves, or maybe it's the knowledge that she finally has some choice other than a dress that makes her shake her head. Maybe it's both.

After a while, Ky asks, "So what is the issue, love?"

"There's no issue! They're all very beautiful-"

"But there is something wrong. You can tell me."

"I love these dresses, but I don't feel quite comfortable in them. I'm not the smallest person in the world and when I walk the inside of my thighs rub together and after a bit it gets uncomfortable."

"Ah, and what else?"

"I think that's it."

"Uh-uh. I can see in your eyes."

Persephone can get away with nothing down here. How to put into words that indescribable feeling of being a girl but not always feeling totally like one? How to put into words that she wants to wear these dresses but sometimes once they're on her body she feels like an imposter and just a little out of place?

"I don't always feel very feminine," she relents. "Or I do, but then I put on things like this," she gestures to the canary-yellow gown Ky has thrown over the screen, "and it doesn't feel right even though it's beautiful and I love it."

"I know something about not feeling one way or another," Ky says.

"Everything okay?" Hades calls from the sitting area on the other side.

"Yes, nosy!" Ky calls back. "So tell me which garment was your favorite so far. As far as just how it looks."

Persephone points out a spring green dress she tried on a few minutes ago. The bodice has ribbon wrapped around it almost like bandages, with thin straps that fall off the shoulder. It isn't as poofy as some of the other ones, and silk leaves trickle down the skirts.

"A great choice," Ky flashes a smile and then disappears with the dress, leaving Persephone in her underthings.

"Where did they run off to?" Hades asks from across the screen. She sounds closer than before. Maybe she's getting impatient.

"No idea."

"Have you found one yet?" Persephone had stopped stepping out to show her the garments a bit ago out of frustration

"I'm not sure- oh."

Ky is back with the green dress, but it's changed. A lot.

"Put these on." They hand her silky, high-waisted beige shorts and a matching band to go around her breasts. She has to take off the breast garment she came in to put on the new one, but she's allowed to pull the shorts over her underwear.

"Arms up," they demand and slip the dress over her head. As they go around to lace up the back, Persephone audibly gasps at her reflection. Ky has taken out much of the skirts to leave a simple, sheer layer that reveals her legs underneath. The bust is the same, the pale breast band showing underneath the layer of jade chiffon. Ky left the silk leaves in place, scattered over the bodice and descending the skirts to her bare feet.

She can't pinpoint what exactly about it feels so much better than it did before, but it's like she's let out a breath she didn't know she'd been holding.

"I. Love. It. Thank you so much, Ky."

They peek over her shoulder at her reflection. "It's an honor. When you don't fit the mold, you learn to get creative with it." They wink at her. "Now go out there and show her before she combusts from impatience."

Persephone takes a moment to steady herself, not used to showing so much skin even if it's still beneath fabric, and steps out.

Hades stops pacing and stares at her. From the crown of her head to the tips of her toes Hades takes her in.

"Perfect," she says.

Persephone beams.

CHAPTER 10

Though she tries to ignore it, the word rings in her head for the rest of the evening. As Hades pays for the dress, and as she purchases a deliciously warm and flaky cinnamon pastry from a stand outside. As they walk back to the castle, Persephone holding the parcel of her dress close to her body as if someone will jump out of the dark trees and take it from her, taunt her and say she should have known it was all too good to be true. As Hades leaves her once more at her door frame to prepare for the ball. As Sofia gently swipes a bit of red on her cheeks and lips, and a stick of kohl on the lid of her eyes.

"How did she manage to organize a ball in a matter of hours?" Persephone asks Sofia.

Sofia chuckles. "She has her ways. And it's been so long since we've had dancing here, I'm sure everyone was eager to help."

Persephone chews on her lip, debating on whether or not her next question will get her into trouble.

"Is she...good to people?" She meets Sofia's eyes in the mirror.

Sofia smiles, gently. "Very much so. She can be dark and intimidating, but she is kind. Why, what have you heard of her?"

"Not much, I'm afraid." Yes, she'd heard of a dark king. She'd heard some tell of torturing souls, of black pits where the dead are kept weeping and in pain.

"Are you?" Sophia brushes Persephone's hair behind her shoulders. "Afraid?"

Yes, she thinks. But she instead says, "I'm not sure."

"Hades never brings guests down here, did you know that?"

Persephone shakes her head.

"So I'd say, Miss Persephone, that she might be just as scared as you are."

"I doubt that," she replies, fiddling with the rings on her fingers that Hades had lent her. "So what's going to happen tonight? I've never been to a ball."

Sofia grins. "You are going to love it."

Sofia helps her into her dress and gives her a pair of gilt sandals to wear, with straps twining up her legs to below her knees.

"Look at yourself," Sofia urges, nodding toward the floor-length mirror. Persephone intends on just glancing but when she sees her reflection she can't help but stare. Her cheeks are pink. The green of her dress brings out the green and gold of her eyes, which are brighter than they've been in a while. She feels beautiful. She is beautiful.

"Oh," she breathes.

Not a second later, there comes a knock at the door that makes her heart stutter. She knows it's her.

"Ready?" Sofia asks, and Persephone nods.

Sofia opens the door wide, and Hades is in the hall with her hands on her hips. Persephone nearly gasps when she sees her. She's certainly dressed up for the event. The black velvet of her brocade has gold threaded through it in small vines all over. Its collar is high, and she has a sweeping cape that is black on the outside and gold on the inside. She wears a ring on each finger, and studs with a looped chain along her ears. Her hair looks a bit curlier than usual and swept back.

They stare at each other for a second, before Sofia interrupts with a soft, "Uh-hmm."

Hades snaps out of her reverie first. "Are you ready?"

"Yes." Persephone feels nerves eating away at her stomach.

"Then let's go." Hades says it a little gruffly, offering the crook of her arm to Persephone. She takes it, and as they walk silently down the corridor she can't help but run her thumb over the soft velvet covering Hades' bicep.

"Are you going to dance?" Persephone asks quietly, anything to interrupt the silence.

"I don't usually."

"Will I be expected to dance?"

"You may do whatever you please."

"Will there be food?"

This breaks Hades' hard exterior, and she laughs.

"What's funny?"

"Nothing, it's just. You seem so anxious but then you ask about food."

"I always need a snack."

"We have plenty of those."

They reach a part of the castle Persephone's never been to before. In front of them stands huge oak doors. Persephone can hear the music thrumming through the walls and stone floors underfoot, strings of all kinds and something that sounds like an organ, blowing deep. And the laughter and chatter of hordes of people.

"That sounds like a lot of people," she says.

"It is. Nearly the whole kingdom came here to meet you."

"Meet me?"

Hades nods. "This celebration is for you, after all."

Suddenly Persephone feels flushed.

"What if they don't like me?"

"They'll tear you apart limb from limb and suck the marrow from your bones."

She whips around to face Hades only to see her suppressing a smile.

"That is not funny!"

"No one will dislike you. And if they do, they're wrong." She nods once to her as if checking again that everything is as it should be and coming up satisfied. "Let's go."

At that, the doors swing open and outward of their own volition and Hades walks her into the cavernous chamber on the other side. At their arrival, the revelry falls silent. The crowds separate on either side of them. Persephone can feel a thousand eyes on her. Maybe more, because some beings down here have more eyes than she does. Nevertheless, she keeps her back straight and her eyes forward. That is until she catches sight of the garlands crisscrossing the ceiling. Lavender petals fall from the garlands here and there, loosened by the lanterns hanging from them. A few of those glowing bugs have found their way in here, fluttering about amongst the flowers. Everything is awash in warm, yellow light from a large stone fire pit in the center of the room. Her mouth drops open as she surveys her surroundings, forgetting for a second that she doesn't want to seem soft.

Hades walks to the far end of the room, where there is a long table atop a dais. A large, throne-like chair sits at the center, with slightly smaller ones lined the rest. It's similar to the one in the throne room, but not as ornate. She leads Persephone there, pulling out the chair immediately to her left for her, and sits at the big chair after she sits. As soon as their bottoms hit the seat, the revelry resumes. Persephone's eyes widen at the range of food on the table. Her favorite - the honey butter rolls was placed directly in front of her spot.

"Whoa," she breathes.

"Tea?" Hades asks and pours her a cup when she nods.

Persephone looks out upon the crowd as they dance and talk and laugh. Children play tag and hide and seek beneath tables and behind their parents' legs. Couples twirl around the fire pit to the beat of the melody. Friends are seated together at various tables, eating and talking. And everyone, absolutely everyone, is dressed so beautifully that at some points it borders on garish.

She sips the tea slowly, not taking her eyes off of the scene before her. She's never seen anything like it. And she's sitting at the head of it all. For a split second, she imagines herself as lord of the underworld. That this crowd of people is her people that she has sworn to take care of. But the reality is that she is unsure of her status here. Hades is treating her as a consort, almost. She wonders if that's what the revelers think.

"You're thinking hard," Hades' voice comes from her right side.

"Who am I to these people?"

"My guest. Our guest."

"Our?"

"Mine and my kingdom."

"What does being a guest mean, exactly?"

"You've never had guests?"

"Of course I have," she huffs. "You're being obtuse on purpose."

Hades shrugs and pops some sort of fruit in her mouth. Perhaps something adjacent to a raspberry, Persephone guesses, as the red-purple from the juice stains her lips. What was she thinking about?

Persephone scowls at her, almost certain she's trying to distract her from this line of questioning. But why?

Before she can delve back in, someone approaches the table. She looks to be a few years older than Persephone, with dark hair cut at the jawline. She's wearing a midnight blue suit of sorts. The collar plunges to her navel, lined with constellations in silver thread. Her pants are the same velvet material, loose at the ankle and dotted with tiny stars. Her eyes are bright hazel.

"So, it's you we have to thank for this party," the

woman says, a smile lifting the corner of her lips.

"Minthe, this is Persephone. Persephone - Minthe," Hades gestures back and forth.

"Hello," Persephone says, shy - again. Everyone in the underworld seems so debonair compared to her.

"Do you want to dance?" Minthe asks.

"Oh, I don't know any dances."

"I'll lead. Don't worry."

"O-Okay."

"Hades, may I steal her away for a dance?"

"If the lady says so." Hades frowns, but it's playful. "Don't be too long, though. She's my guest"

"I thought you said I was the kingdom's guest," Persephone butts in.

Minthe laughs at that. "She's afraid I'll steal you away forever. I might have to, with the dress you have on."

Persephone blushes profusely. Hades gives Minthe a look that Persephone can't interpret and Minthe nods.

"Let's go," she says and leads Persephone to the dance floor by the hand.

Persephone has danced with a girl - Lila - a few times before. Sometimes at village festivals when they had snuck a few too many sips of rum they would twirl together around the village square, laughing and stumbling. The elders would just shake their heads, but Persephone knew they did the same when they were younger. Persephone remembers the feeling of Lila's waist beneath her hands, soft and warm. This time, her partner has a little more hardness and litheness. Minthe places one of Persephone's hands on her shoulder, and with the other holds Persephone's hand. She's warm like Lila was. She's in charge like Lila was not.

As the music swells to something upbeat, Persephone focuses on following Minthe's steps without stepping on her toes.

"It's rude to stare at the ground instead of looking at your dance partner, you know," she says, teasing.

"I'm trying not to step on you," Persephone glances up, and in that split second manages to scuff the tip of her shoe against Minthe's boot. "See?"

"You have to trust yourself. Dancing is much easier than you think."

"Easy to say when you don't have two left feet."

"Look at me."

"I'll step on you."

"It's okay if you do."

Persephone finally looks up and Minthe grins.

"It's instinctual. You'll get it." Minthe spins them both gracefully around the fire as if she were built for dancing. "So what brings you here?"

"To the underworld?"

She nods.

"Um, I got into a bit of trouble." Persephone narrowly escapes stepping on Minthe's boot again, but something about Minthe's expression won't let her look down. "And Hades helped me out of it." Persephone looks over at Hades. She's watching them, face impassive. She's tall upon the throne, lounging with her chin atop her fist. Every bit the formidable god she's rumored to be.

"You're from the mortal realm, right?"

"Yes. I...I sort of made a deal with her. To come down here. And I didn't have anywhere else to go at the time."

"Interesting. What kind of deal?"

Persephone isn't sure if she should tell her or not. Minthe seems genuine, but perhaps that's just the charisma. She isn't sure how many people should know she doesn't have power. It's been taken advantage of before.

"She'd help me become stronger if I came down here with her."

"And you just left? Anyone back home?"

"I didn't 'just leave.' I was in a pretty difficult situation. And my mother is back home."

"Does she know you're here?"

"I sent her a letter, so I should hear back from her any day now."

Minthe nods.

"Are you judging me?" Persephone accuses. The song is slowing to a stop.

"No. I don't know what you've gone through. I'm glad you're here now, though. We'll take care of you." she winks and looks over Persephone's shoulder.

Persephone can sense Hades' presence before she even says, "My turn."

"I'll see you later," Minthe says, and disentangles herself from Persephone. Persephone turns around to Hades and before her waist can feel the cold from the absence of Minthe's hands, Hades' hands are there to replace them. Another tune starts up, a little slower than the one before.

"I'm not used to having more than one dance partner in a night," Persephone muses, but she's flattered. Hades' hold is firm on her. Not too hard, but enough to make her feel that if she were to fall apart, she would hold her together just nicely.

"I have a feeling many more will ask you before the night is over," Hades grumbles.

She laughs. "Are you jealous?"

"What if I am?"

"I don't understand the intrigue. I'm not that interesting."

"Hush."

And hush she does. The quiet between them as they dance isn't at all uncomfortable. It's peaceful. It's nice. Persephone finds it easier and easier to follow Hades' steps as they go, the firelight flashing off of the golden threads in her shirt. Their movement is slow and sweeping, lulling in a way. The overhead glow has dimmed, and Persephone notices that there are minuscule flecks of gold in her dress, all over the fabric of the bust and skirt, and all down the vines. She thought she would feel more self-conscious about the sheer bottom half of the dress, her legs hazy but exposed beneath. But some of the other people here are wearing even less than she. And even if they weren't, here in the arms of a queen, she feels beautiful.

She notices suddenly that the other couples have walked off to the side, that they are the only ones left dancing. And nearly every person in the room is watching them in earnest. People with antlers, people with claws, people with wings, people with tails. Even the musicians are staring at them even as they pluck their strings. It makes a slight shiver roll up her spine.

"Hades," she whispers. "Why are they all staring?"

She hums noncommittally and pulls her closer.

"Hades."

"I've been waiting for you a long time, princess." Her lips brush over Persephone's temple. "We all have."

"What do you mean, waiting?"

"I was looking for you everywhere. She thought she could hide you from me."

"What? Who?"

"Your mother of course. Who else?"

"What do you mean 'hide me'?"

"Exactly as I said. You belong here, Persephone, can't you feel it?"

She can only stare at her, aghast.

"Your mother didn't like that. She wanted you all for herself. Clipped your wings. But you are more powerful than she knows. Than you know."

"Why are you talking like this?"

"Because I think it's time you finally knew who you are."

"And you can't speak more plainly? You couldn't have said any of this sooner? Maybe when there weren't hundreds of people looking at us?"

"That's why I'm telling you now. Every person in this room knows who you are. Every person in this room wants you here."

Persephone begins to pull away now, caring less and less about making a scene. Hades lets her pull back a bit, but holds her there by her elbows. Persephone's shaking her head and breathing a little quicker and hisses, "What are you saying?"

"We were meant to meet. This was meant to happen. You are meant to stay here, with me. And you would be so loved-"

"Stop." Persephone begins to feel a little faint and slips her arms from Hades' grip. Stumbles backward. "Stop!"

"You don't believe me? Maybe it's time you speak to your mother."

"I did! I wrote to her but-" Her blood runs cold. "But I didn't hear back. Did you stop that letter?"

Hades stays silent, eyes betraying nothing.

"Did you?!"

"She would have convinced you to leave, she wouldn't have let you learn how to use your power-"

"I can't believe this."

"She can't protect you as I can."

"From what? Aetius? An overbearing monarch with too much power and control issues?" She's raising her voice now, and she can feel, more than see, the crowd shrinking back from the couple. "That sounds familiar, doesn't it."

Hades flinches.

Persephone can't do this. She turns around and walks out the door, and through another and another, not registering where she is going until the cool air caresses her face and she sees stars above.

CHAPTER 11

She finds herself at the entrance of the garden. She kicks off her shoes and runs farther in, not caring where. She just has to get away from everything in there. She has to outrun it, somehow.

The plant life turns toward her as she goes, reaching for her. She tries to pay it no mind. Through the winding path among bushes and trees and flowers and vines and stone she goes, grateful for the coolness on her skin and the easy movement of her garments.

She finally stops when she reaches what seems to be the end of the garden. It's a pitch-black thicket of trees, all grown so close together that the branches overhead intertwine to almost form a roof. She figures no one will find her here, and steps into the woods. Everything alters immediately. The air turns biting and she can no longer see the faint glow of the castle's windows. She has left relative safety. Whatever. Let something come and try to claw her apart and gnaw on her bones. She's in no mood to be messed with.

She huffs and plops down with her back against a tree. And promptly begins to cry. It's a trait of hers she's always hated. Anger comes out as tears, sadness comes out as tears, and happiness, as well, comes out as tears.

And when she's feeling one emotion, she's feeling all of them. What is the point of anything, if the people in her hometown want to kill her and her mother may not even know where she is and the one person who is helping her is also keeping things from her and she hasn't even come into her full power yet. Why is she here? In this dress, in this realm, in this existence? And what is there to do about it? She doesn't want to die, necessarily. She is just tired. She sits there for what feels like hours, but she knows it must only be half an hour or so.

The wind picks up, cooling the wet tracks down her cheeks. Her skin prickles from the cold, and something else. Something is watching her. She tenses, cursing herself. This is what she gets for turning into a blubbering mess. She should have known not to show weakness here.

She rises slowly, scanning the vicinity. There is only darkness on all sides. Should she stay still? Should she run? She's fortunate enough to have come across very few predators in the wild. The only thing she knows is that the snakes in her and her mother's garden don't like any sudden movements. And as for predators not in the wild, don't make eye contact.

She puts one foot in front of the other as gently as she can. The brush crackles with each step, poking the soles of her feet. Act like nothing's wrong. Like you're just strolling back home.

She walks a while like this, but she can still feel whatever is encroaching from behind. She has to fight the urge to look behind her, not sure if she wants to see it. Somehow she knows that if she can make it back into the garden proper she'll be safe. Her chest tightens when she sees the break in the trees that means the palace grounds are up ahead and it takes every bit of her willpower not to sprint the last bit of distance to safety, like she would do as a child, blowing out the candle in the kitchen and running upstairs as fast as she can.

She's maybe five steps away from the clearing when she

hears a clicking behind her. Something zips by in her vision and sets itself in front of her, between her and the garden. It's huge and hairy, limbs bending with far more joints than a human would have - and gods it has so many limbs. The shock of it falls away and she is finally able to register what it is, skin gray and dull and eight eyes on its head, all pitch black. A spider. Its mouth is open and panting, putrid breath billowing from behind the largest pincers she's ever seen.

She screams. Stumbles backward. It lets out a sharper clicking sound and scrambles forward. She starts running then, adjacent to the clearing. It follows her, always a step behind and to the right, ensuring that she can't make a break for the clearing without being caught.

Her heart is pounding out of her chest but she knows she can't stop. The feeling is similar to the fear that rose in her as she was being chased out of town. And that makes her angry.

It manages to hook a furry leg around one of her ankles and yank her down. She lands on her stomach, the breath knocked out of her. The barbs on its legs tear into her skin and she screams again, flipping over on her back to face it.

It hovers over her, and then something odd happens. Its face twitches, and suddenly it's Aetius with eight black eyes and pincers, sprinkling spittle in her face. As she scrambles to get away, its barbs sink deeper and she feels warm blood gushing down her leg. It clicks again, twitches, and it's her mother. Demeter's beautiful face is drawn into a snarl and dotted with too many eyes. Something ice-cold comes over Persephone.

"No," she hisses. "No, no, no." And there's a staticky feeling in her gut and her hands and something shifts within her- the creature widens its pincers - her mother face split open in a facsimile of a smile - and lunges for her neck - and then everything explodes. It never reaches her throat. She can hear its squeals of pain, its grunts of struggle, but it's nothing compared to the power surging through her. Roots have erupted from the earth to slither around the creature's neck, thorns have grown around each of its limbs and then more are circling its head, piercing its eyes and cutting into the abyss of its mouth. It screams and thrashes as it's pulled away from her, and then down, down, down. The movement of all the plant life around has loosened the soil enough for it to be pulled slowly and agonizingly into the earth. It tries in vain to drag her down with it, but a swipe of a particularly thorny vine slices its leg so deep that it releases her. The barbs sting as they pull out of her skin, but she doesn't scream. She stands, watching as vines and dirt fill its screaming mouth and crusts its eyes and it goes farther and farther down until she can't see a single leg anymore.

Then everything goes still. It's over. She looks around to see daisies and marigolds and daffodils have popped up all around her and the scene. She exhales, shaking, and collapses onto the ground. It's so very quiet. It's so very cold. She can't stop trembling. She's sitting for a minute or two when footfalls come crashing through the underbrush, and she can sense to whom they belong, somehow.

"Persephone." It's Hades. She's panting, wide eyed, as if she'd run all the way here from the castle.

She steps over the vines and stems to the center of the floral explosion, to Persephone. She doesn't look at Hades, arms around her knees and eyes fixed on the flowers. Hades kneels.

She takes Persephone's hand and lifts it to her mouth. Persephone looks at her then. Hades' lips brush over her knuckles, petal-soft. She huffs warm breath onto her frigid skin.

"What was that?" Persephone's words come out in a rasp.

"One of the more unsavory creatures that haunt this forest. I didn't think you'd come out here, or I would have warned you." She surveys the land around them, the deep gauges in the earth that the thing's legs left, the colorful mess of stems and petals scattered and tangled. "But it looks like you handled it."

"Barely."

Hades releases her hand to unclasp something at her neck, and then her cape is wrapped around Persephone. It's warm from her body. Persephone feels tucked in.

"There are safeguards-" Hades looks over at the clearing. "There are safeguards to keep things out of the garden, but not keep things in."

"Why not?"

A soft frown comes over her handsome face. In Persephone's fatigued state, she wants to reach out and unfurrow her brow. She doesn't. "No one is a prisoner here."

"You shouldn't have done that."

"You're talking about the letter?"

"Yes."

"I shouldn't have."

"Don't do it again. If no one is a prisoner here, don't do it again."

"I won't."

Persephone scours her face for any sign of dishonesty or anger or disappointment. Hades sighs.

"No, Persephone. I may be selfish and hedonistic, but I never want to hurt you. I'm sorry."

Persephone pulls the cape tighter around herself.

"Why does this keep happening?" she asks.

"What? Me making an ass of myself?"

Persephone huffs out a laugh. She isn't even sure what she means.

"Did I ruin the ball?" She fiddles with the hem of Hades' cloak, running the silk between her pointer and thumb over and over again.

"No. It's probably the most excitement we've seen here in a long time. I was overeager. I put a lot on you at one time and at the wrong time. But Persephone, seeing you in that dress, in my home, looking for all the world like the most beautiful thing I've ever seen, I..." Hades trails off, then shakes her head.

Persephone's cheeks burn. "Will you explain it all to me?"

"Of course."

"Maybe tomorrow? I'm tired."

"Of course, princess."

She can't even muster the energy to quirk her eyebrow at the endearment. Instead, she accepts the fluttering of her stomach.

Persephone shuffles around in preparation for standing up, and her ankle pops out from beneath the cloak. She can see Hades' face change the instant she sees her wound. Three jagged lines in her flesh still bleed a bit. They're deeper than she thought.

"Why didn't you tell me you were injured?" Hades demands, eyes flashing.

"I forgot." It's true. In the face of all that had happened, her injury had completely taken a backburner.

"Forgot? Gods, Persephone." The hem of her dress slips down and Hades pulls it back up, away from the wound. "Can you walk?"

"I'm sure I can."

She doesn't look like she believes her. She helps Persephone up, but standing puts enough pressure on the wound that she hisses.

"May I?" Hades asks.

Persephone looks her in the face, in the depths of those chocolate brown eyes, and sighs. "I'm heavy."

"I'm strong."

Persephone cringes at the thought of being picked up, to have someone else bear her weight, but she's not sure how else to get back to the castle. "Since you keep making an ass of yourself it's the least you can do." She replies, deadpan. She can tell by Hades' flinch that it pains her.

"Yes ma'am." After Persephone wraps her arm around Hades' shoulders, she lifts her into her arms. She holds her close to her chest as she walks through the trees.

"I was joking, you know," Persephone says, resting her head against Hades' shoulder.

"May I tend to your wound or shall I call Sofia?" When Hades speaks, Persephone can feel the slight rumble in her chest. She doesn't miss her changing the subject, but doesn't comment on it.

"I don't want to bother her. She may still be at the party."

Hades nods.

When they get back to Persephone's room, Hades wastes no time in setting her on the edge of the bed, commanding her to stay still as she leaves to gather medical supplies.

She comes back with gauze, a cloth and basin of water, and some sort of poultice in a jar. It's purple and gooey and smells a bit like mint. She drags a chair over from beside the fireplace and sits across from Persephone, lifting her leg into her lap.

She works methodically, quietly. Washes the dirt and dried blood away with the cloth, dragging it gently over Persephone's skin. It barely hurts until it's time to apply the poultice.

"This will sting," Hades says and dips two fingers in the jar. And sting, it did. She spreads it on the wound a little at a time, glancing now and then at Persephone's fists balled in the coverlet. After a few seconds, the concoction becomes a cooling sensation, and Persephone sighs in relief. Then comes the gauze, wrapped snugly without putting too much pressure on the cuts.

"Done," Hades says. Persephone expects her to lift her foot off of her lap, but she holds her ankle lightly, thumb tracing over the arch of her foot.

"Thank you."

"You're welcome."

Persephone likes this, the two of them in her bedroom. Quiet and warm in the flickering of her fireplace.

"Hey. I used my power."

Hades cracks a grin. "You did."

"Now I have to figure out how to do it when my life is not in danger."

"Ready for another lesson tomorrow?"

"Yes. Will you send my letter?"

"I already did."

Persephone nods, something like electricity shooting through her nerves. She's anxious. What will her mother think? Will she be angry? Surely she'll respond, right? She and her mother rarely fight, but she has seen the force of her mother's fury upon others.

Then she yawns.

This time Hades does lift her foot from her lap and sets it down gently.

"Goodnight, Persephone."

"Goodnight."

Persephone slips into a blessedly dreamless sleep.

CHAPTER 12

Training begins the next morning in earnest. It's like the lid that sealed Persephone's power away has popped off. Hades asks her to summon a sunflower, right there in the training room. She accidentally summons forty. Forty sunflowers nearly as tall as the ceiling.

Persephone shrieks when they rupture through the floorboards. There's a beat of silence, then Hades bursts out laughing. She can't help but join in.

Next, she is supposed to summon vines to restrain Hades' hands as she pretends to come at her as an attacker would.

"I don't want to hurt you," Persephone protests.

"It'll be fine."

Hades lifts the wooden sword they've been training with and acts as if she will slice her in the midsection, and she ducks away from it.

"Are you sure?"

"More sure than I've ever been in my life."

Hades is in such a strangely good mood that it's infected her as well. Hades swings the sword again, towards Persephone's neck.

She calls the vines. Unfortunately, it's with all the force

she has because she doesn't know how to moderate her demands quite yet. They come out of the walls and the ceiling as well as the floor, twining around Hades' limbs until she's suspended in mid-air, arms raised above her head.

Persephone gasps. "I'm so sorry! I didn't mean to!"

"It's okay. Now let me down."

An idea comes into Persephone's head.

"I don't know how to make them go away."

"Then cut them away."

She acts as if she's thinking about it for a moment.

"I'm not sure I will."

"Persephone." There's a hint of warning in Hades' voice, the kind of warning that makes her want to push just a bit more.

"What if I like you at my mercy?" she muses.

Hades narrows her eyes.

"Aren't you a big, strong goddess? Can't you get yourself down?"

Hades positively scowls now, tugging on the restraints.

"It seems your vines are unnaturally strong, dear."

"Use your magic, *dear*."

Persephone relishes in the cut of her eyes towards her.

"Get me down. Now."

"What's wrong?"

"Get. Me. Down."

"Are they really immune to your power?"

Hades speaks through gritted teeth, "It would seem so, yes."

Persephone can't help the wide grin that breaks across her face. She's just never felt more powerful in her life. Here she is, a novice at best, subduing an actual god.

"Okay," she says, and rushes over to the wall to grab an actual sword to cut vines with. But as soon as she touches the green skin of one, they all fall away.

"Oof-" Hades drops to the floor like a stone.

Persephone drops the sword and kneels beside her

body, which is sprawled out on the training mat. "Are you okay?"

"Yes." Hades' eyes are closed.

"I didn't mean to do that - I was going to cut them-"

"I know." the ghost of a smile comes over her face. "I think you're the most powerful individual I've ever met."

"Now you're just joking."

"I'm not." Hades sits upright. "Your power can resist mine. That isn't normal. Do you know what that means?"

"No?"

"It means that if we worked together, we'd be unstoppable."

CHAPTER 13

Demeter comes home to an empty house. Nothing seems amiss, except for a vase that was knocked on its side. It sits right beside the stairs, before the entranceway. It's as if someone was in a hurry to leave and knocked it over. The main thing wrong with her home is that Persephone is not there. She doesn't even call out her name when she steps inside, that's how much she can feel it. Her daughter is not in this realm.

Zymi is sitting beside a piece of parchment on the table, which Demeter sees has her name written on it. It's an envelope. She tears it open and finds a letter from her daughter.

Demeter feels as if there is a stone in her chest. This is not happening. She won't allow this to happen. She was never close to Hades, but she knows enough. Knows all too well how the gods are destructive and selfish and hedonistic. She crumples the letter in her fist, jaw clenched.

At that moment, two unfortunate guards bang on her front door.

"Open up! We know you're in there," they yell.

"What do you want?" She calls back, calm as can be.

Inside she feels as if lava is churning.

"The prince requires an audience with you."

An audience. With the prince that her daughter stabbed, for a good reason, Persephone promises. Demeter worries what that reason is, more than she's worried about her daughter stabbing him.

She swings open the door, and the two guards stumble back. "She escaped?"

"Yes. But you won't."

They lunge towards her but suddenly there are wheat grains in their lungs - they splutter and cough and tears roll down their faces, and when they finally fall to their knees Demeter makes the wheat disappear.

They stare up at her, horror written on their faces.

"Take me to the prince then. I expect to hear exactly how she escaped."

"Will you help bring her back to me?" an arrogant voice calls out. She looks up and sees the face of Aetius peeking outside of his carriage. Coward.

She narrows her eyes.

"I'm getting her back. After you tell me what happened."

She sits across from him at a long table, face unchanging and Aetius tells her what his guards saw. Even some of the guards themselves come to describe what they witnessed. And she seethes. Oh, how she seethes.

Aetius is obviously omitting the full reason why Persephone chose to stab him. But the audacity of him to then hunt her down like she was an animal. She's proud her daughter kept running, but part of her wishes she had hidden in the woods, waited for her to come save her.

The worst of it all is who had taken her. Hades. Of all the gods that could have fulfilled the damned prophecy, it was the god of the underworld. A dark, dank place too miserable for her daughter to ever step foot in. Hades better be behaving. Hades better be afraid of Demeter.

YOUR EYES AS HONEY

After the prince and his guards tell her the full story, she rises from her chair and promptly walks out. A few of the guards begin to protest - she is supposed to be detained for the crimes of her daughter, after all - stop in their tracks when she whips around, eyes blazing at them. They'd seen, or heard, of what happened to their peers. They have good enough sense to avoid the same fate.

"I'll deal with you later," she promises Aetius and walks out the door. It's been a while since she's spoken to any other celestial beings, or used her powers for anything major. She'll be a bit rusty. But she will find a way into the underworld.

CHAPTER 14

Persephone had thought perhaps people would look at her differently after the outburst at the ball, but the biggest change is that now *everyone* smiles or nods at her when they see her, or both. Not that folks weren't friendly before, but now...well, now she feels seen. Welcome. Accepted. In a way she's never felt before. Which she didn't expect seeing as she had a public argument with their queen.

People speak to her more now. She makes a few friends at dinner one night. A group of young women around her age is talking about their favorite bookshop in the village, and her ears perk up. She can't help but ask if it was the one in which she saw books flying when Hades had taken her to get a dress. They reply that it's the same. Their names are Ismeni, Zina, and Voleta. They invite her to come to the village with her sometime and she nods, grinning. Friends! People who want to be around her! It's been years since she's had a solid friend.

Training goes well. Better than she ever could have hoped for. Now that her power's unleashed, she feels so much better. The dark circles under her eyes have faded somewhat, and her face has stopped being so sallow. She's always been plump, but the good eating in the underworld has given her more curves.

One day, while she and Hades are taking a break from her training, she asks something that's been on her mind.

"Why is my power suddenly here, do you think?"

"It's not all the way here, yet. You still haven't had the big breakthrough."

She thinks back to the vines around Aetius's throat, the ones dragging that monster into the earth.

"You mean, there's more?"

"Yes. It'll be huge. You won't be able to miss it."

"And that's when I'll know I've fully come into it?"

"Yep."

Persephone takes a sip of water from her cup. There's a pitcher of water in the training room today, as they've been practicing more combat-related movements. She finally relented that it might be useful to have simple hand-to-hand combat lessons as well as lessons for her power. It's difficult to take such a strong woman down, and she's suspicious that Hades lets her get the upper hand sometimes, but it's very fun.

"How do I get there?" she asks. The quicker she comes into her full power, the quicker she can see her home again. Her mother. Zymi. Her beloved meadow. No one will be able to harm her.

"It's different for everyone. Something just clicks."

Persephone frowns. Patience has never been a virtue of hers.

"You'll get there," Hades says. "What are you in such a hurry for?"

Persephone looks at her, incredulous. "I miss home."

Hades quiet for a moment. "Which part do you miss the most?"

"My mother. My cat."

"Tell me about your cat."

"He's fat and beautiful and stupid and my best friend."

Hades rubs her hand over her mouth, obviously trying

to hide a smile.

"What? It's true. I love him so much."

"No, I understand. I have a pet, as well."

"You do?" she perks up at this.

"Yes. He's rather large but very sweet."

"What kind of pet is he? Can I meet him?"

"If you can get through five more drills without complaining, then yes. I will take you to see him."

Persephone agrees and jumps up that very second to get the drills over with. Hades shakes her head and joins her.

A while later they're finally done training for the day, and Persephone couldn't be more grateful. Hades walks with her out of the castle and onto the grounds, and it looks like they'll be heading through a path in the forest again. Persephone's trying not to pant too obviously, beads of sweat trickling down her spine. Hades had taken the last five drills very seriously, moving towards her faster than before and with more force. She managed to land a blow on Persephone's arm with her staff, but it never hurts. Hades, for the most part, seems unruffled.

They take a different path today, opposite the direction of the village. Persephone notices the sky is a lot brighter today than she's ever seen it. It's like evening is just setting in, though she knows it has to be early afternoon. She comments on it, but Hades doesn't seem concerned about it. No one else in the castle seems to be, either, even though Hades had said it's never happened before. Almost like they were expecting it. And then the things Hades said at the ball...it sent a shiver through her.

The path is more winding and thorny than the other one. Spindly trees with black bark reach out towards her. It reminds her of the creatures lurking in the depths. She speeds up to match Hades' pace.

"The thing that attacked me...I suspect there are more of them?"

"Yes," she replies. "But you're safe. They won't bother you while you're with me."

"How can you be sure?"

Hades gives her a look that serves to remind her just exactly who Hades is.

"Okay," she relents and looks away.

"You are afraid. I can nearly hear your pulse."

When Persephone doesn't respond, Hades slips her hand in hers. It's an instant tether, and Persephone *knows* intrinsically that she's protected. She holds her hand tight and sidles closer.

They walk in silence for a few more minutes, then up ahead, there is an opening - a massive archway of naked branches and thorns. It's probably twice as tall as Persephone. She gasps when they step through.

In front of them is a huge, slate wall. It goes so far up that it seems to extend into the sky, farther than Persephone can see. It's so wide that she can't see the ends of it. Oddly, she didn't see it up ahead as they were walking through the forest. There must be some sort of illusion or enchantment that conceals it until you're right in front of it. Set into the stone wall is a gigantic, ornate gate of black iron. Beyond it, one can only see mist. However, the most surprising thing about the scene is the three-headed hound that sleeps in front of it. If she thought the spider-creature was big - the dog-creature is five times that. She wonders warily if there are any animals in the underworld that are actually proportional.

Hades whistles and the three heads pop up. The dog lumbers to its feet, nearly as tall as the gate. It stretches a bit, one of the heads yawning wide so that Persephone can see the rows of razor-sharp teeth in each mouth. Then it bounds over to where they stand as if it is a mere puppy, shaking the earth they stand on. Persephone hides partially behind Hades' shoulder.

The animal doesn't attack. Instead, it sits right in front of them, tail wagging. The middle head lowers so that

Hades can give it scratches, and then the other two are fighting for attention.

"Hey there," she coos. "My good boys."

She turns to Persephone. "Would you like to pet them?"

"I didn't think your pet would be so big."

"Yeah. They're sweet though."

They do look pretty cute, teeth aside. They have long, black fur and big brown eyes. Not unlike Hades.

Persephone holds her hand out, trying not to let it shake, and the three heads instantly turn toward it and sniff it. Then one pokes its big tongue out and licks it. Though not fond of the slobber, Persephone feels affection spark in her for the creature.

"What's his name, or is it *their* names? How many dogs is this?"

"Cerberus is their official name. But this one is Bunny," Hades pats the head on the far left, "this is Bear," the middle, "and this is Bumble. As in Bumblebee," the far right.

"Why have an official name if you don't call them that?" Persephone asks. She smiles to herself when Bumble leans into her scratches.

"They guard the gate. They have to sound intimidating. And I'm not entirely sure if they're technically one dog or three. I found them as puppies in the forest. I believe they had been abandoned by their mother or had gotten separated somehow. Anyway, they wouldn't have survived like this in the mortal world so I brought them down here with me."

"And they grew into this?"

"I helped a bit. A little magic here and there, and a whole lot of training."

"You kind of resemble each other," she muses.

Hades shrugs. "They're my little guys."

"I wouldn't use the word little, but they're very sweet." Cerberus's fur is silky soft underneath Persephone's palm.

"Do they get cold out here? Do you ever let them inside?"

"They're no longer mortal. They're tough and have a job to do."

"Not even during Yuletide?"

"We don't celebrate that. But sometimes on the winter solstice, they'll sleep by the fire in my room."

Bumble scratches his ear, leg thump-thump-thumping the earth.

"It's nice to meet you," Persephone tells them. They look at her, tongues hanging out. "Such a vicious guard you have, Hades."

"I know," she says fondly.

At dinner, Persephone brings up going to the village with Ismeni, Voleta, and Zina. Not exactly asking permission, per se. Just wanting to schedule it around their training. Hades is happy she's made friends and encourages her to go. Persephone's not sure what she expected, but she's pleased nonetheless. But then she remembers the last time she ventured out without Hades, and the still-healing slices on her calf.

"I won't meet another one of those things, will I? You say nothing will happen to me while I'm with you, but I won't be with you."

"I've got some business to attend to in the village anyway. I'll run my errands while you have fun. Those creatures don't tend to stray near the pathways, anyway."

"Do I need to be chaperoned?"

"No. I have friends too, you know. Things to do."

"Who?" she asks, quirking her eyebrow.

"Ky. Minthe. Sophia. Tari."

"Most of them work for you. Maybe all of them, I don't know what Minthe does."

"We work *with* each other, thank you. And Minthe helps with important matters around the realm."

"Such as…"

"Afterlife affairs. Restless souls who try to crawl out of

the acid pit, rowdy spirits disturbing the peace in the fields of asphodel."

Persephone gapes at her. Then it dawns on her she's never asked how, exactly, things work around here. She's been too busy either training or trying to survive in general to really think about the fact that she is in the realm of the dead.

"How are all these people here, anyway? I thought the underworld was for dead people."

Hades chews on her steak for a second. "You remember what I told you about Cerberus?"

She nods.

"Certain souls who die before their time, who were wronged, who never had a happy, full life, I give them a second chance."

"What do you mean?"

"I give them a choice. Pass on into the fields to rest in peace, or continue to live. Here."

"Am I the only person alive here?"

"Everyone here is alive. You're just the only person here who hasn't died before."

"That's why everyone likes you so much."

"I do have charm, too. That helps."

"Sure you do."

Hades throws a roll at her, which bounces off of her head and into her soup. She stares at her, mouth wide open, but Hades just laughs.

CHAPTER 15

Demeter is standing in a creek near the meadow where her daughter was last seen, twirling a coin between her fingers. It's been a while since she used this particular power, and she's rusty. But she focuses, fingernails biting into her palms, thinking only of her intent. The sun shines on the creek and she throws a palm-full of water into the air, making it shimmer all the hues of the rainbow.

"Iris," Demeter calls. The water suspends in the air, becoming mist. The rainbow ripples and there's a sound like wind chimes on a close neighbor's porch, comforting and kindred. The mist comes back together to form the shape of a woman. She becomes more solid by the second, this creature with glimmering skin and pale, opal-colored eyes. Her hair is the color of clouds, curling around her plump face.

"Demeter," she says. Her voice is deep and rushes out like water over stones in the creek bed. "It's been a long time."

"I need to speak with Hades."

"I'm doing fine, by the way. Thank you for asking. It's lovely to see you again too," Iris examines her nails as she speaks.

"I don't have time for this. Hades took her."

"Took who?"

"Persephone."

"Oh."

"Connect me to Hades - please, Iris."

"Yes, yes. I will. But you should visit us sometime. Olympus misses you."

"I doubt that. Hurry, please."

Iris frowns. "You know, Hades is nothing like Zeus-"

"IRIS. I have given you your payment, now let me speak with her."

Iris looks at Demeter for a moment, and Demeter can see the disappointment on her face. Iris was once a close friend, but she can't afford to waste these seconds.

"The mortal world has changed you," Iris says. Then with a wave of her hand, she steps back into the mist and disappears. The colors warp and wobble for a second, and then another figure begins to take shape. Tall, broad, dressed all in black. It clears and she's staring at Hades, who is staring at her. She can't see anything around Hades, just her standing in the mist over the creek.

"Demeter."

"I swear if you've laid a hand on her I will make your life even more miserable than it already is."

"I assume you speak of Persephone."

"Don't play dumb with me," her voice is frigid. She hasn't felt this kind of rage in decades. "Bring her back to me *now*."

"She chose to come here. And she'll choose when to go back."

"What have you done? How did you even find her?"

"She called to me. She summoned me to help her."

"Nonsense. Let me speak to her."

"She's not here right now, she's out with some friends. Having a wonderful time and learning how to use her powers, might I add. The things she should have been doing her entire life."

"You're lying. You have her locked up somewhere-"

"I promise you, she's safe and sound."

"I don't believe you. I have to see her."

"Okay," Hades scratches her jaw. It's such an urbane gesture that Demeter is momentarily snapped out of her anger. It comes rushing back in soon, with the strength of a tidal wave. "I'll bring her up to speak with you tomorrow."

"*Now.*"

"Believe it or not, I am a busy woman. And she's *not here right now.* It will be tomorrow unless Persephone says differently."

"Whatever you're doing, it stops now. She is not yours."

"But she's yours?"

"Yes," Demeter snarls.

"And you know what's best for her?"

"Of course."

"And you think cutting her off from her power and hiding her from the rest of the world is best for her?"

"It worked until now, didn't it?"

Hades steps closer. "And did you, for one second, think about what she would want? Did you ever ask her?"

"Don't you dare judge me. I did what I had to so she'd be protected."

"What exactly are you protecting her from, Demeter? When I found her she had a split lip and was seconds away from being torn apart by an angry mob." She's speaking faster and louder than before.

"I didn't know she was hurt."

"Probably because you weren't there. If you're going to render your daughter defenseless, the least you can do is make sure she isn't alone."

That reignites her. "Who are you to tell me how to take care of her? All you have is that miserable pit you call a kingdom. Everyone around you is already dead. You know nothing of loving another person, of protecting them. My daughter and I are none of your business, so stay. Out. Of. It."

"Unfortunately for you, it is my business. Why do you think she called to me, and not any of the other deities? Not to Zeus, not to you?"

"She doesn't even know how-"

"But she did it anyway. And it was me. It will always be me."

"What, you believe the fates deigned to give you a soulmate? Least of all her? She's of the flowers. That girl is pure sunlight. You're nothing but death and rot and darkness. Whatever you think is happening, it's not. You just want someone to drag down with you because you're lonely, and I won't let her be that someone. You can't have her."

"I already do." Hades waves her hand and her image disappears, the mist falling back to the creek.

Demeter's heart is racing. Her fists tremble, clenched by her sides. She will talk with her daughter tomorrow, and make her see reason. She'll come home. Demeter knows she will. And she will not be going back down there, ever.

.

CHAPTER 16

Persephone is walking beside Ismeni in the village square, Zina and Voleta in front of them. She finds she likes being around them very much, and even though they were friends before they met her she doesn't feel excluded.

They had gone to the bookstore they had spoken about at dinner, and she had a blast dodging volumes as they flew by. Most of them were still like books in the mortal world, but some hopped or sang or hid from you.

Persephone asked Voleta why the books flew, hoping she wouldn't think she was stupid. Voleta was kinder than Persephone thought she would be, given her devastatingly beautiful face. She explained that some authors enchanted their books, giving them life like any other living creature. It also meant that it was very difficult for anyone to destroy a copy, since the moment one sensed danger it would fly out of their hands.

There were spell books, history books, cookbooks, love stories, epic tales, and horror books. She was amazed. There is no such selection in the small mortal village she's from. In the end, she picked up a history volume. One that spoke specifically about the tales of the gods. She's determined to learn, despite her mother's best efforts. And she figures Hades probably doesn't have enough time to fill her in on all the details of the celestial sphere.

They're at the fountain in the middle of the square, munching on some kind of jelly-filled fried dough and watching the dim sunlight reflect off of the fishes' scales in the basin when Minthe appears behind them. Hades had been in the village as well, doing whatever business he felt the need to do with Minthe in tow, letting Persephone spend time with her new friends. Now Hades is nowhere to be seen. Minthe's face is serious, calm on the outside, though Persephone has been sensitive enough all her life to detect others' moods and can tell something has happened.

"Sorry to interrupt, ladies, but I must escort our princess back to the castle."

"What's wrong?" Persephone asks.

"I'll tell you on the way."

Worry threads through her stomach as she gathers her one shopping bag and bids the girls goodbye.

As soon as they are out of earshot, Minthe says, "Your mother is not very happy you're down here." She walks with her hands in her trouser pockets, casual.

Persephone's heart drops. "Is she here?"

"No. She spoke to Hades, though, and is demanding your immediate return."

"How did she speak to him if she isn't here?"

"Iris - the messenger god. If she has a bit of water she can connect anyone, anywhere to each other."

Persephone tucks that piece of information away to process later. "And she demands my return?"

Minthe nods.

"I can't go back yet, surely Hades told her that."

"Demeter seems to believe she's snatched you away from the mortal world and is holding you prisoner."

"I bet Aetius lied to her."

"Who?"

"The mortal prince that I stabbed."

"Yikes." Minthe shakes her head but doesn't prod. "Either way, she won't listen to Hades and the fact that she couldn't speak to you at that moment made her angrier."

A thousand emotions flicker in and out. Anxiety, excitement, happiness, guilt. A lot of guilt. Persephone can't go back there right now, she'll know that. She has to.

"Hey there princess, take a breath." Minthe puts her hand on Persephone's shoulder. Persephone hadn't even noticed she'd been on the verge of hyperventilating, but all the signs are there. Heart pounding. Lightheaded. Tight chest. "Are you okay?"

Persephone nods, though she's not sure. It's her mother, though. Everything will be fine. Her mother will make everything fine.

Persephone doesn't notice how she doesn't have to follow Minthe to know how to get back to the castle. How she's memorized the route and how used to being here she is. How the fading sun shines across her hair. The sun that she summoned, unwittingly.

As soon as they step into the front entrance, it's dead silent. Like there's not a single person in the entire world.

"I believe Hades is in the throne room," Minthe murmurs to Persephone. "Do you know how to get there?"

She nods, and Minthe slips away.

She tries to calm her breathing on the way there with little success. She pushes open the big doors to find Hades sitting on the throne, elbow on the armrest, pinching the bridge of her nose. Her mother must have been *very* angry then.

Hades looks up when she hears Persephone's footsteps.

"Hello, flower."

"Hi." She stops a few feet away.

"Your mother is a very determined woman."

"She is."

"I know now where you get it from." She gives a half-hearted laugh. "She thinks you're being held captive, or that I've put a spell on you. She wanted to speak with you and didn't believe me when I said you were out with friends."

"I'm sorry. Did she seem very angry at me?"

"Don't apologize. You're her only daughter, it's understandable. I don't know if she is angry at you, but she is angry in general. And at me, especially."

"I need to speak with her."

"Yes, you do. I can take you tomorrow."

Persephone is partially relieved that she has time before facing her mother. It means she'll have more time to worry. Worry about what her mother will say to her, what she will say to her mother, how she will explain stabbing the prince, what the prince has said to her, if she will make her stay in the mortal realm.

"Okay." Persephone nods. "Thank you. Will we go the same way as last time?"

"Yes, we will be taking the carriage."

"Great," Persephone says, remembering the terrifying dizzy-sickness of traveling between realms. "Wait, won't that attract too much attention?"

"Perhaps you're right. We'll go another way, then."

"How?"

"You'll see."

It turns out Hades can shadow-hop. She doesn't like the term when Persephone first says it and insists there's no hopping involved, but how else is she supposed to describe stepping into one shadow, feeling yourself go weightless, soaring in pitch black, only to pop up in another shadow miles and miles away. The entire experience lasts less than five seconds, and Persephone is a bit annoyed that Hades didn't use this method when she first went down to the Underworld.

"They needed to be terrified," Hades explains. As if the sight of her wasn't frightening enough, in all black with dark, shadowy tendrils curling around her. As if she isn't one with the darkness itself.

They appear in the shadow of a tree right outside her meadow. Persephone chose this place because it was far enough away from the village that she wouldn't be seen, but close enough for her mother to meet her without much difficulty.

As soon as she sees her mother break through the trees on the other side of the meadow, Persephone feels some kind of weight in her chest lift. Not all of it, but some. This is her mother. Her safety. She half-runs across the meadow to throw her arms around her, taking in the scent of her. Baking bread and the sharp aroma of green tomato vines. Her mother's arms come around her as well, holding tightly.

Oh, how Persephone missed her. Demeter pulls away all too soon. She holds Persephone at arm's length, examining her from head to toe.

"Are you hurt? Are you okay? Did Hades do anything to you?" The demands come rapidly.

"No, I'm fine! I'm fine!"

"Good. Let's go." Demeter grabs Persephone's hand and begins pulling towards the village, away from Hades.

"Wait!"

"You can tell me on the way home."

"No, stop!"

"Enough, Persephone."

"Listen to your daughter, Demeter," comes Hades' cold voice. It stops Demeter in her tracks.

She turns her head slowly. "You don't command me, Hades. You barely command anything."

While her mother is distracted, Persephone manages to pull her hand out of her grasp.

"I can't go back there, mother. They'll kill me."

"Like hell, they will. I'm here to protect you now, and

I'm never leaving you again."

"You shouldn't have to do that, though. I need to be able to defend myself!"

"And you thought running into the arms of the first god that showed you interest was defending yourself?"

Persephone winces, taking a step back. The elation that came with seeing her mother again has dissipated.

"I don't know how it happened. I didn't even really mean to."

"Didn't mean to what? Run away with one of the most dangerous deities in all the realms?"

"She might be dead if she hadn't," says Hades.

"You shut your mouth."

"It's true, Demeter. Though I know you hate to hear it."

Persephone gleans that they've met before, and she knows logically that her mother used to be in the celestial sphere, but just how much history do they have, she wonders.

As if Hades reads her mind, she tells her "You know your mother used to be a lot more involved in celestial matters before she had you and hid you away."

"I SAID STOP TALKING!" Demeter bursts.

Persephone shrinks back even more. She's confused and upset and she wanted to see her mother but not like this.

"You had no right," her mother seethes, advancing toward Hades with her finger pointed. "You had no right to take her! What's happened is none of your business. You were born to be alone and you will always be."

"Mother," Persephone whispers.

Hades comes closer. "And who do you have besides your precious daughter? A daughter that just had to physically pull away from you? Please, enlighten me."

"You're miserable. And intolerable. And you will never get near her again."

"Please stop," Persephone says, but it's quiet.

"She doesn't want to go with you and that frightens you. Maybe if you were able to protect her, or better yet, teach her, this wouldn't have happened-"

"I AM protecting her! From you! From all of them!"

"STOP!" Persephone screams. And with the shout comes a burst of thorns, belladonna and dahlia and thistle, stretching all around her like tangled spokes on a wheel.

Everyone goes silent. Instead of the shock Persephone thought her mother would have, there is just a pinched expression on her face.

"Listen to me. I can't go back yet. You don't know what happened, what I did. They'll string me up or worse," her voice starts shaky but gains strength as she speaks. "I've finally got some power. I've been waiting my entire life for this. Hades saved me, mother."

"I see," Demeter says. "You'd choose her over me? After all I've done for you? *I* could help you."

"That's what you got out of that? That I'm choosing her over you?"

"It's what it feels like."

"All I want is to never be powerless again."

"You don't need power. You have me." And the conviction with which Demeter says it sparks something in Persephone's mind. Something dark and twisted that tastes like betrayal and Persephone tries to shove it away.

"Do you even care that I stabbed the prince?"

"Of course!"

"But you care about that less than you care about whatever grudge you have against the gods."

"No. I never said that."

"You didn't have to."

"Well then tell me," Demeter says, with a tinge of exasperation. "Whatever happened between you and the prince? Because he's more than ready to forgive you."

And at that moment, Persephone feels so profoundly let down by her mother. Or perhaps it's her own fault for putting her mother on a pedestal in the first place. Part of her wishes she had never attacked Aetius, had stayed quiet, had gone along with everything, and married him so she would still have that unbreakable relationship with her mother. That safety in her. She doesn't feel so safe around her now. That old fear rises again, the fear she thought she'd squashed. The fear of her mother hating her for what happened. Hating her and blaming her and casting her away. She can't help it.

"Tell me, love. I'll listen." And though Demeter seems genuine, Persephone can't do it. She can't tell her mother.

At that moment, the sound of warrior yells fill the meadow and armed men stream out of the forest behind Demeter. Aetius's men.

Persephone stumbles backwards and Hades wraps an arm around her waist tight.

Demeter closes her eyes and pinches the bridge of her nose. "You were supposed to wait, your highness." She calls out, and Aetius comes from behind a tree. Coward, Persephone thinks. He's on his white horse big enough to trample the three of them standing in the meadow.

"Mom?" Persephone whispers. She doesn't want to believe it but what choice does she have? Her heart is pounding like a racehorse and she's breaking out in a cold sweat. There is lead in the space her stomach once inhabited.

"Persephone," Aetius says. "We've been worried sick about you."

"You do not speak to her," Hades growls, and a hush falls over the entire meadow. She steps in front of Persephone, blocking Aetius's view of her. She is grateful. She doesn't want Aetius to see her shaking.

"You don't understand, milady." Milady? It must be taking every ounce of acting in his body to place himself below another person. "We've had a misunderstanding, and I must apologize to her."

Persephone startles as black shadows curl out from Hades' palms, creeping towards Aetius as he speaks.

"Stop!" Demeter yells. "You will let him speak." She flexes her fist and vines begin to crawl out of the ground. But as soon as the shadows touch the vines, they wither and crumble.

Hades, quietly and over her shoulder, asks Persephone, "Would you like to hear the version of the story he has told people? Or shall we leave?"

"I'll hear it." And perhaps by hearing it, she will understand her mother better.

"Speak then," Hades calls to Aetius. "You have ten seconds."

"That's hardly enough-"

"Then you'd better start. One."

"I came to her house to propose to her-"

"Two."

"And when I professed my love-"

"Three."

"She became enraged. She thinks-"

"Four."

"I only want her for her power, but-"

"Five."

"That couldn't be further from the truth!"

"Six."

"She stabbed me and left me for dead-"

"Seven."

"But I still love her. And wish to-"

"Eight."

"Make her my wife. How could I-"

"Nine."

"Want her power? She has none."

"Ten."

"Persephone, come home. We know what's best for you," Aetius says, as if he and her mother are a unit. As if he's her family. "I know she's had some issues in the past with her…behavior. But I'm willing to overlook that. And I am sincerely apologetic if I caused any offense with my proposal."

"What part of ten seconds don't you understand?" Hades says.

"Persephone, honey," Demeter says, craning around Hades' form to see her daughter. "He's not angry with you. You can come home."

Home. The word sounds foreign to her now.

"Move aside and let me speak to my daughter."

"So you can take her with you back to the little village? And make her marry this pathetic excuse for a man?"

"I'm not making her do anything! You're the one…"

Persephone tunes it all out. Demeter and Hades begin yelling in earnest now. Demeter must have had enough, because she raises her hands and suddenly vines jump for Hades' throat. With a wave of Hades' hand, they are chopped in half. Demeter doesn't give up. Vines are whipping back and forth across the space between them, only to be met with shadows.

Persephone keeps backing up. If only she could die right there and then, and none of this would have to happen anymore. It would all go away with her.

While Hades and Demeter are distracted, Aetius slides off his horse carefully and makes his way over to Persephone. He grabs her arm hard and hisses into her hair, "Marry me and I won't kill you. You can't hide from me forever."

She cringes away from his putrid breath and sharp words, struggling to free her arm. "Get away from me," she screams. Aetius releases her and steps back a second before her mother and Hades turn their heads. Hades storms over, shadows pulsing around her frame. She's nearly apocalyptic.

She grips Aetius's throat and hoists him in the air. He kicks and scratches at the hand around his neck, face turning purple, sputtering and gasping. His men notch arrows in their bows and launch them at Hades, only for them to dissolve in the shadows around her. Demeter just looks bored at the theatrics.

YOUR EYES AS HONEY

After an amount of time that Persephone deems appropriate, she taps Hades on the shoulder. She looks at her, nostrils flaring. Like she's death incarnate.

"Can we go home?"

"Let me kill him first."

"No. I want to be the one to do it, but I can't today."

"Are you sure?"

"Yes."

Hades drops Aetius and he hits the ground like a sack of potatoes.

Persephone slips her hand into Hades', and doesn't look back as they walk back to the other side of the meadow, to the darker part of the forest. Hades must feel her hand trembling because she squeezes it with her own. Persephone walks away with her, even as her mother screams her name. Even as she tries to grow vines around their ankles to stop them, Hades waves a hand and they fall off. Persephone can hear her mother running after them, but it's too late. They step into the shadows of the trees, and are gone.

CHAPTER 17

Persephone sleeps through the night and wakes up the next morning with eyes puffy and red from crying. She'd rather wrap herself in the cocoon of her blankets and never speak to another person again, but she knows someone would come looking for her. She stays in her bathtub until her fingers start to wrinkle and picks the most comfortable garment in her closet, a loose, flowy gown with poofy sleeves. It's soft against her skin and as light as the morning air. And morning it is - it seems the sun has risen finally to the height it would be in the mortal world at this time.

She feels new and old at the same time. She wanders into the kitchen and finds a few people bustling around, making pastries and bacon and eggs. One older gentleman is chopping strawberries, Persephone's favorite. They nod at her as she comes in, and when she approaches the gentleman he greets her with a good morning.

"May I chop them up?" she asks. He shrugs and hands her the knife, wandering off to find another task. It's methodical and comforting, the steady thunk-thunk-thunk of the knife when it hits the chopping board. Every once in a while she pops a slice in her mouth, savoring the sour-sweet burst on her tongue.

"Do these grow in the underworld?" she asks one of the other women. A plump, beautiful girl with black hair down her back.

"No. Her Highness requested they be picked from up above and brought down today."

"Does she have a particular fondness for them, then?"

"Not that I know of, but you do." The woman says it matter-of-factly.

Persephone plucks another slice from one of the bowls. "Yes," she murmurs. "I do."

"Hello," Persephone greets Hades when she sits at the table.

"Good morning. You're not usually here this early," Hades says.

"I helped set the table this morning." The assortment of colors down the table is picturesque. Bowls full of fruit, cupcakes with delicate icing patterns, steaming pies, meat from the skillets, and porridge line the table runner. She made sure to keep the largest bowl of strawberries near herself. "Thank you for these, by the way."

Hades frowns. "Who told you?"

"Someone in the kitchen. Do you like them?"

"I don't know. I'm not in the mortal world very often."

"Here." She pinches a slice between her thumb and forefinger, holding it to Hades' lips.

"Are you trying to feed me?"

She rolls her eyes and pulls her hand away to eat the slice herself, but Hades holds her wrist.

"No, I'll take it." And take it, she does. Gingerly between her teeth, eyes on Persephone's. It makes her heart stutter. If they were not in front of so many people she thinks Hades might have licked the juice from her fingers. She didn't mean for the simple gesture to turn into something so intimate but Hades has a way of burrowing under her defenses and making her blush.

"What do you think?" Persephone asks, vaguely irritated that she sounds so breathless.

"The best thing I've ever tasted."

"Really?"

She nods. Persephone can see mischief dancing in her eyes. She tries to ignore it and not embarrass herself any further. She picks up a croissant and begins spreading jam on it.

"You're adorable when you're flustered," Hades says, chin resting on her fist.

That only serves to fluster her more. She huffs. "You're irritating."

"You're beautiful."

Persephone can only shake her head. "Eat your breakfast, dammit!"

After a few minutes, the amount of people in the dining hall thins out.

"How are you today?" Hades asks, all traces of humor gone from her voice and face.

There are only three other folks at the table, far away enough as to not hear their sovereign's conversation.

"I'm here." Persephone shrugs.

"Do you need a day off from training?"

"No, I'm fine."

"You're fine."

"Mm-hmm."

"That was quite a use of power yesterday."

"Yeah. I don't know how that happened. I didn't even think about it."

"You were stressed and upset. It's understandable."

She pushes oatmeal around her plate, but doesn't eat it.

"No one will ever hurt you like that again, Persephone."

She freezes.

"I won't let it happen."

Her chest feels like it's slowly constricting, perhaps in a

good way or perhaps not. It's so hard to tell.

"You don't know what happened."

"I can guess. And my guess is correct, is it not?"

She stares at her plate.

"I'll be in the training room. Come whenever you're ready." Hades gets out of her seat and gathers up her dishes to take to the kitchen.

"If you don't mind me asking, what 'behavioral issues' was he talking about?" Hades breaks the silence of the training room. They had been meditating, Hades deciding that Persephone's use of power yesterday was enough to go easy on her today, no matter what she says.

"It was just something from when I was younger. I was very angry." She still is.

"Probably because you were so pent up from not being able to use your power."

"You might be right." She had never considered that, but she's already had too many revelations recently. She packs it away to examine later.

"So what did you do?"

Persephone sighed. It's not something she liked to think about a lot. It's partially why she was a social pariah in the village.

"I did a lot of things."

"Like?"

"I once bit a teacher's hand." She's interrupted by the sound of low laughter. "She was snapping her fingers in front of my face. I zoned out a lot in class. Not because it was boring, I just did. Still do sometimes."

"I'll make a note to never snap my fingers at you."

"I punched a boy in the face one time because he said some not very nice things about a new girl in the village. He ran home to his mommy and she made sure I couldn't attend the summer solstice party with the other kids. But it's okay because the girl became my best friend, for a while."

"I see. For a while?"

"Her family moved to another village."

"She couldn't stay if she wanted to?"

"She was unwed. Still the property of her father, in the mortal realm."

"Disgusting."

"Very."

"Any other instances of these so-called anger issues?"

"Yes. I screamed at her father, in public."

"That's not that bad."

"It is in the mortal world. A woman is never to yell, especially at a man. We are supposed to be quiet and polite and demure every second of every day."

"What did he do to anger you?"

"It was right after I found out he was moving them to another village. And I found out the reason he was doing so was because of me. Because I was unnatural and unladylike and corrupting his daughter."

Hades waits for her to elaborate, and Persephone sighs.

"When we shared beds as little girls it was cute. Not so much when we were eighteen. He found us once," she swallows, the memory as vivid and painful as the day it happened. "We had broken into his rum stores and were tipsy in the barn. We were kissing."

Hades still looks confused.

"He wanted his daughter to marry a man."

"Why?"

"To carry on the family legacy."

"It doesn't require a man to do that-"

"He didn't see it that way."

"So he chose to move his entire family away because of that."

"Yes. And Lila, in her efforts to please her father, didn't stand up for herself. I haven't seen her since."

"She didn't stand up for you either."

"I suppose not."

"Do you still love her?"

"Yes. But not as a lover, not anymore. If I ever did. I think we got so close that the lines between types of love blurred together."

"You could see her again if you wanted."

Persephone looks into her face and sees the sincerity there. Even though it could threaten whatever they have together, she would still give her that.

"I'm not sure she'd want to see me, or I, her."

Hades nods, solemn.

Eager to change the subject, Persephone asks, "Have you ever loved a man?"

"Yes. I have had lovers of all kinds."

She does her best to fight the flare of jealousy that rises and almost regrets asking. "Anyone I know?"

"No. A fae here, a nymph there. A demigod, for about a month."

"Wow."

"What?"

"You have significantly more experience than me."

"I've been alive for a while. What else am I supposed to do down here? Knit?"

Persephone laughs. "That's exactly what you're supposed to do."

"Duly noted. I'll have a sweater for you by the end of the month."

CHAPTER 18

Persephone's days are pretty standard for the next week. Wake up, eat breakfast, train, eat lunch, train, read the book she got from the shop, walk in the garden, eat dinner, bathe, go to sleep. She wants to write to her mother, but it's also the last thing she wants to do. She misses that connection, the version of her mother she thought would never betray her in such a way. And the worst part is that Demeter doesn't see it as a betrayal. It makes her wonder about other things regarding her mother, things she would never have dared to think about before coming down here.

The most pervasive, gut-wrenching thought is that her mother didn't want her to develop her powers. Hades said something about her mother keeping her hidden. It would be so much easier to keep a daughter hidden if the daughter didn't show signs of being celestial.

All of those reassurances and platitudes when Persephone was upset, the way her mother always seemed so unbothered by Persephone's lack of power. And when she thinks about it, did her mother try to help her develop it? She didn't do much other than stroke her hair and tell her to look within herself, to 'feel the earth.'

For the first time in her life, Persephone is disappointed in her mother. It's an uncomfortable feeling, mixed with guilt borne of two decades of worshipping her mother. She'd sacrificed so much for Persephone to have a good life, right? She extricated herself from the celestial sphere completely to protect Persephone. Protect her from what, exactly? And how much of a sacrifice is it when she hates the other gods?

These questions swirl in Persephone's head even as she does menial tasks. She's taken to helping cook breakfast when she can. There's a rotating cast of cooks, so there must be a schedule or something. They all welcome her with plenty of tasks and small talk. One morning Zina has kitchen duty and she hums while rolling out dough. Intrigued by the melody, Persephone asks her what she's singing. It turns out to be a bawdy pub song with lyrics to make a sailor blush. It makes Persephone laugh, though. And for the rest of the morning, they sing while they work, to the chagrin of some of the older people.

The bit of brightness eases the rest of Persephone's morning. She talks with the others at breakfast, getting to know some of the other residents of the castle. She waits and waits for Hades to arrive, good mood deflating by the second. When she's the last one at the table she gives up and takes her dishes to the kitchen.

Persephone heads to the training room, hoping Hades won't stand her up there too. She is proven wrong. After thirty minutes of stretching and warming up, she goes out in search of her. Persephone doubts she overslept, and even if she did Persephone will not encroach on such intimate territory as her bedroom. She'd be thoroughly offended if Hades skipped breakfast and training to read in the library or walk in the garden, so she doesn't look there. And then she realizes that there are too many rooms in the castle for Hades to be hiding from her in. But there's one place she told her not to go - the throne room. That has to be where she's at.

Persephone creeps down the corridors until she reaches the large doors to the throne room. They are closed, but she puts her eye to the middle to see if she can see anything. She can vaguely make out Hades' form on the throne. She's sitting up straight, hands on the armrests. She is wearing her crown.

Before the dais upon which the throne rests is a figure on their knees. From the back, it looks to be an older man, frail and shaking. He is speaking but it's too muffled for her to make out the words. He's pleading, the tempo of his sentences rattling faster and faster. Hades puts a hand up to silence him. She says something, to which the man responds. Hades lowers her voice. The cadence of her speech is much more imperious than Persephone is used to, then the man begins weeping. Persephone's heart begins to pound. Is this a villager? Or has she caught Hades in the middle of judging a soul? What could he have done?

With a wave of Hades' hand, the man begins to scream. Then his body dissolves into thin air. Persephone covers her mouth. She begins to back away from the door, but it looks like Hades is staring straight at the doors now. As if she can tell she is there.

"Persephone," Hades speaks, loud and clear. Damn.

She has to open the door now. Has to face what she's witnessed.

She steps into the room, unsure if she's afraid or nervous or both. It's at least ten degrees colder here than in the hallway.

"What are you doing here?" Hades sounds tired, and not at all pleased.

"You didn't show up for breakfast or training."

"I told Minthe to relay my apologies, I'm busy today."

"I haven't seen her."

"Of course you haven't." She pinches the bridge of her nose. "Tell me, what is the point of having employees who don't do what you ask them to do?"

"Why are you busy? Who was that man?"

Hades leans forward in her seat, elbows on her knees.

"Come here," she murmurs, beckoning Persephone. She steps forward slowly, footfalls echoing in the chamber. Hades keeps beckoning her until she's standing a foot away from her.

Moving slowly, giving her time to retreat or tell her to stop, Hades places her hands on Persephone's hips. She has a flash of insecurity - she has never been slim and weight has always gathered around her hips and stomach - but Hades' dark eyes staring up at her, nearly black, kills any protest she may have. Hades is looking at Persephone as if she's the only thing in the world that matters. The press of her palms against Persephone's sides feels grounding rather than constricting.

"You, little flower," Persephone allows Hades to pull her closer so that she's standing in between her knees. "Are very distracting. You've caused me to neglect my duties."

Persephone aches to twine her fingers through Hades' hair. It would be so easy to do so, but she resists. She's on the verge of learning more about this mysterious woman, and though she speaks of Persephone distracting her, a few touches from her have nearly distracted Persephone from what she just saw. "What exactly are your duties?"

Hades cocks her head, no doubt still perplexed at how little she knows. "Judging souls. Sending them to whichever portion of the underworld to which they belong."

"And where did that man go?"

"Tartarus."

"What is that?"

"A place for the worst of evils. Most go there and suffer until they've burned their transgressions off, but some stain forever."

"What did he do?"

"Inherited a fortune from his father. Exploited the

labor of those less fortunate than him, paid them hideously when he did decide to pay them, and refused to help when asked. He died rich, but hated."

"There are plenty of men like that."

"And they will all suffer the same fate."

She thinks of the old man's wail before he dissipated into thin air. He seemed so fragile. But then she thinks of the hungry bellies of some of the children in her village. She and her mother would bring them vegetables from their garden frequently, but the gauntness that comes from inadequate clothing and poor housing and parents too overworked to properly care for them never goes away.

"And what of the good people?"

"Fields of Elysium. Eternal peace."

"That doesn't seem possible."

Hades draws her closer. "It is."

"Where do you think I will go?"

"You will not die."

"You'll stop me?"

"You forget you are a goddess. And even if you do die, I don't know that I would let you go."

She looks away, blush rising in her face. "What about normal people? Who are neither very good nor very bad?"

"Fields of Asphodel. It's not so different from the mortal world."

"Eternal mediocrity?"

"It's what they choose to make of it. A blank canvas."

"Sounds like a second chance."

Hades shrugs. "Sounds like you're distracting me once again from my very important work."

"Sorry."

"You don't sound very sorry."

Persephone shrugs in turn, but doesn't make to leave. "Do you like your duties?"

"What an odd question."

"Not really."

Hades sits back, letting go of her waist. She misses the

warmth instantly.

"It's not something I necessarily choose to do. It just *is*."

"If you could do anything, what would you do?"

"I *can* do anything."

"You know what I mean. If you didn't have to do this."

Hades scratches her chin. "Believe it or not, I like giving people what they deserve. I like sending good people somewhere they will be happy and I like sending bad people somewhere they will be miserable. Not by the ethics that your mortal juries use, but by the ones that are universal. I may be a god of wealth, but I care not for it. I don't hoard it. Hoarders of wealth in the mortal world get rewarded. I like the fear in their eyes when they realize my code of ethics is different." She leans close to her. "When they realize they'll be damned."

Persephone listens with rapt attention.

"Do you think that makes me a bad person?" Hades has a glint in her eye that she can't decipher.

And she doesn't know the answer to the question. But she likes this side of her, dark and vengeful and commanding and looking at her like she's the only thing she cares about. She likes it because Hades is right and unlike those who ruled over her in the mortal realm, she protects rather than treads upon her people.

Persephone leans over her, placing her hands on the armrests of the throne. There's something fiery inside her chest, delicious. Hades looks up at her, eyes flitting from her lips to her eyes.

"I don't think I care," Persephone says.

Up close, she sees bits of amber in the brown of Hades' eyes.

She leans in slowly, examining her face. She looks so serious, a slight furrow in her brow and her plush lips almost pouty. Persephone imagines the soft pink of them pressed to her own and how good it would feel to have Hades melded against her. Her entire being. Before

Persephone loses the nerve or can make herself feel guilty for wanting this, she closes the gap between them. A jolt runs through her when her lips meet Hades'. Like something is righting itself, falling into place. It's magnetic. Hades' hands come up to her face, her thumbs stroking along the curve of her cheeks, and the rest of her fingers slip into her hair. It feels incredible. The wet heat of her mouth on Persephone's. The surety with which she holds her. The way she smells even better up close, all pine and a hint of spice. She wants to collapse against her on the throne and let her have her any which way she wants. Let her hold Persephone's body with the same tenderness she holds her face.

Someone knocks on the door behind them.

Persephone pulls away like she's been burned.

Hades calls out, "Yes?" from the throne, but she's looking at Persephone. She doesn't dare move under her gaze.

"Just reminding you, milord, that there are souls waiting for your judgment," calls a muffled voice from the other side. It's Tari.

Persephone feels her cheeks heat up. Does Tari know she's in here? Does he know what they've been doing?

Hades groans and swipes a hand over her face. "One second," she calls back.

She rises from the throne and puts a hand at the small of Persephone's back. "Come on, little flower."

Persephone's sheepish and guilty and embarrassed. Has she really just kissed her? Was it so bad that she has to be kicked out of the throne room?

Hades stops before the double doors and pulls her close. She rests her forehead against Persephone's which is an intimacy that she has never experienced before. She fights the instinct to pull back because really, she likes this closeness.

"Remember when I forbade you from coming here?"

She nods.

"It was because I didn't want you to be frightened. Of what I do. Of me. Are you frightened?"

"Not of what you do."

"Of me?"

She thinks for a moment before she answers, "Not in an entirely bad way." While it's scary to be this truthful, this vulnerable, it feels okay with her.

Hades silent, then presses her lips to Persephone's forehead. "Remind me to thank Minthe."

"For?"

"Forgetting to tell you I'm busy today."

She laughs and Hades presses another quick kiss to her temple, then sends her on her way.

CHAPTER 19

Persephone feels like she's floating through the corridors. She hates comparing everything she experiences with Hades to things Aetius did, but she can't help it. It's such a stark difference, this comfortable excitement she has now. It's a feeling she didn't know was possible. Aetius would attack her mouth with his own and she could do nothing but stay silent and bear it until he decided he was done. It was sloppy and gross and suffocating. She and Lila had shared a few tipsy kisses in their teenage years. They were very soft and quick. They felt great, these little bits of affection stolen in the hayloft of Lila's family barn or by the bonfire of a young people's party in the woods at night. She looks back upon them fondly. But what she did with Hades felt brand new and ancient at the same time. Being able to effectively tame one of the most feared and powerful gods in all the realms. And having that god bring out the wild in herself.

She decides to go back to the training room and practice on her own. She's been able to successfully summon her power for nearly a week now. After long lessons, she'll go back to rooms and collapse in a deep nap for an hour or so. It's like drawing something from inside her, at the same time it's drawing from the exterior world. Either way, the tugging can be just as exhausting as it is rewarding. For the next few hours, she summons rings of sunflowers around her. With each ring, they grow taller and taller until she can no longer see the walls of the training room, until the skylight is blocked out and she's wreathed in shadow. She sits in that pocket of darkness for a bit and feels cocooned.

She comes back from training sweaty from the effort and other physical exercises that Hades swears will help her in combat. Her least favorite is pushing herself up from the ground and back again, which makes her arms shake and her cheeks red. But she wouldn't – couldn't be self-conscious while training or she'd never get anything done. Hades doesn't judge her anyway.

As she passes her desk on the way to the washroom, something catches her eye. It's a small piece of parchment with something handwritten on it:

Persephone,

Would you do me the honor of dining privately with me tonight? If so, meet me in the kitchens at seven o'clock. Wear shoes you can walk in.

Yours,

H

Her heart skips a beat. She's been alone plenty with Hades, but dinner alone is something different. More intimate. Where will they walk? She takes the note and slips it into the book on her bedside table, unfolding the dog-eared page she had previously used as a bookmark.

A half-hour before their meeting time, she slips on her sandals and a comfortable, simple cream-colored dress. It would be comfortable to walk in and she likes the way it frames her chest and collarbones. How silly of her, she muses, to be going on a date with someone days after her life was threatened. And her life is still threatened, but not here. Here she can just be a young person with a crush.

When she gets to the kitchens, Hades is standing at the counter talking with one of the head chefs. She's got on a loose black shirt and trousers, and lace-up boots. It's more casual than Persephone has ever seen her, apart from during training. She smiles when she sees her.

"You came."

"Of course I did." She wonders at how Hades could think she would refuse.

"Great." She picks up a large basket from the counter and the blanket folded on top of it. "Let's go."

"Are we going on a picnic?"

"Perhaps."

"I've never been on a picnic at night."

"Me either."

Hades thanks the chef and they head out the door, through the gardens. It's a clear, crisp night. The flowers perk up as Persephone passes and turn towards her as she leaves as if watching them go. She's reminded of puppies.

It's colder than she expected. She fights the urge to sidle next to Hades and crosses her arms instead.

They chat about what she did for training today, the various exercises Hades will have her do tomorrow, simple things like that as they wind through a trail in the forest. Some of the glowing insects flit through the trees, and small creatures scamper through the dappled moonlight on the underbrush. Eventually, they fall into an easy silence, hearing only the crunching of leaves underfoot and the chirping of bugs, and the low rush of wind. It's peaceful. Nothing like the night she encountered the beast that wore her mother's face.

After hiking up an incline for a few minutes, they walk through a break in the trees to the top of the hill covered in tall grass and clover. Before them sprawls the entire village. It glows with golden light from candles and fireplaces and lanterns.

"It looks so alive," Persephone says. Chill bumps raise on her arms, from the sight or breeze or both.

Hades puts down the blanket and basket and comes up behind her, chin resting atop her head, smoothing her palms from Persephone's shoulders to forearms and back again. "You should have told me you were cold," she scolds. Persephone leans back against her warmth, but she lets go after a few seconds.

Persephone turns around to see her rifling through the basket. Out comes two plates, some covered dishes, some parcels wrapped in white cloth, some bottles and jars, and finally another blanket. She expects Hades to hand it to her but instead, she wraps it around Persephone's shoulders herself. It's dark, soft wool and smells like her.

"Thank you."

"You're welcome." Hades spreads out the other blanket on the ground and gestures for her to sit on it. She wanders into the woods for a minute or two and comes back with an arm full of wood, which she plops a healthy distance away from the blanket and with a flourish of her hand, ignites it.

"I didn't know you could do that!" Persephone exclaims, basking in the heat.

"I haven't done it in a while. Living in the underworld will leave you impervious to the cold."

She sits across from Persephone and arranges the dishes between them. Persephone reaches out to help but she shoos her hands away, insisting she sit there and get cozy. Finally, everything is settled before them. There's seasoned chicken over a bed of greens, some creamy pasta, and of course her favorite bread rolls, still steaming and glistening with butter. Hades pours them both a goblet of sweet wine.

"Thank you for this," Persephone breathes. She can't

remember a time she was treated with such decadence and care.

The firelight flickers over Hades' answering smile, and she takes a swig from her cup.

"What are you waiting for? Dig in."

And dig in, she does. The food is divine, of course. It always is. She can't help but let out a moan when she takes her first bite of chicken, so tender it nearly falls off the bone.

Hades watches her, eating her own meal with patience Persephone doesn't have. She's reminded of an old folk tale the old women in the village would tell the children, of a witch in the woods who would lure kids to her cabin made of sweets, and when the kids ate themselves full she would throw them in the oven to cook and eat. She wonders idly if Hades is fattening her up for something. She doesn't have the look of a witch, though. She has the look of a wolf. Persephone finds she doesn't mind it. It sets her heart aflutter and makes desire curl in the lower parts of her body. She would deny it, of course, if she was accused of sucking the spices off the tips of her fingers for a second longer than necessary. She just doesn't want to miss a taste of this delicious meal, she reasons.

When she's finished, she lies back on the blanket to gaze at the sky.

"I don't understand how you have stars here," she says. "Are they the same ones?"

"Yes, they are."

"But we are underground."

"To get here, you travel beneath the mortal realm, but it is not so different."

"Why are you here?"

Hades' brow furrows, "I'm the queen, my dear."

"I mean why are you here, instead of one of the other gods? Did you choose this?"

"Zeus wanted what he thought would make him the most powerful, and Rhea, our mother, obliged. No one dared to go against her or him, so he got the sky. She gave Poseidon the sea because in her eyes, that was second-best and he was the second-best son. And I got the underworld. I didn't exactly choose it, but we fit together anyway. I like the power that I have. I like that it doesn't come with the attention that the others' powers come with."

"And your father?"

"He is imprisoned. We threw him Tartarus."

"Oh." She is momentarily shocked to silence.

Sensing her unasked questions, Hades continues, "He received a prophecy that one of his children would overthrow him, so he swallowed us one by one after our births. But Rhea tricked him when she birthed Zeus, and hid him away until he was grown enough to take on Kronus. Zeus eventually attacked him and made him empty the contents of his stomach. Hera, Demeter, Hestia, Poseidon, and me. I remember seeing sunlight for the first time."

Hades trails off, and Persephone has no idea what to say. What must Kronus look like, to be able to swallow godlings whole? No wonder no one challenged Zeus, if he saved them. And how him holding something like that over their heads must make them all crazy.

"I wonder why Rhea didn't do it sooner," she says.

"I guess she waited until she got a child worth her time."

Hades stares unblinking at the city below.

"And then after you were freed, you were put right back in darkness."

She turns to look at Persephone. "I learned to like it after some time. Learned to thrive on it. Became it. I know many mortals think I'm evil, but I don't mind. I'll be a villain if I need to."

"In what possible way are you a villain?"

"I sent that man to the pits of hell, regardless of his age or frailty, didn't I?"

"But he hurt others."

"That's not how a lot of people see it. They say two wrongs don't make a right, but I don't believe that. I believe in balance. If you hurt others, you will be hurt. If life doesn't do it before you get to me, and often it doesn't, I'll certainly fix it. People think *that* is cruel."

"The people who think that are often not the ones who were hurt."

"Very true," Hades says and sips her wine.

Persephone aches to take Hades' hand in hers, but she doesn't. Hades may need space, and Persephone knows she's too sensitive to rejection to react appropriately if Hades did pull away.

"I like your darkness," she says.

The corner of Hades' mouth pulls up in the slightest smile. "And I adore yours."

For a second Persephone can see the roguish young god Hades might have been, had she not been sequestered to the dead for eternity. She can see all of the followers she would have, the paramours, the comrades. She imagines that version of Hades getting drunk with her friends and skinny-dipping, as she'd heard of other young people in the village doing. While she mourns for the youth Hades never got to have, she likes her how she is now. All of her flaws and frustrations and beauties mesh into a creature Persephone's fascinated by.

"Enough about the past," Hades says. "It's time for dessert."

She pulls out two more items from the basket. One is a bowl filled with warm, flaky pastries and the other is a little jam jar. She pops open the lid and uses a knife to spread the jam on top of the pastry, and hands it to Persephone.

Persephone thanks her, examining the offering before taking a bite. The flavors instantly burst in her mouth, sweet and buttery and – strawberry!

"Strawberry jam?" she asks, unable to hide her excitement.

Hades nods. "Chef taught me how to make it."

"YOU made this?"

She laughs at Persephone's incredulity.

"I made everything tonight. I enjoy cooking. I don't do it often because I'm busy and I think I make Chef nervous."

"You can be intimidating."

"It's not even that. I like using fire for everything. I think he's afraid I'll burn the kitchens down."

Persephone giggles, taking another bite of the pastry. It almost melts in her mouth. The sweetness of the bread is perfectly balanced by the tangy burst of jam. "This is divine."

"You have a bit of jam on your face."

"What? Where?" She wipes at her chin.

"Here, look at me."

She turns her face toward Hades who leans in close, gently holding her jaw. "Right…here." Then her lips are on her skin, the expanse of cheek nearest the corner of her mouth. Persephone holds her breath. Hades kisses the jam away.

When she pulls back Persephone feels frozen. "Delicious," Hades says.

She looks down to where the pastry rests in Persephone's hands. Persephone hadn't even noticed the tips of her fingers had dipped into the jam on top of the pastry, likely due to Hades distracting her. "You're a messy little thing, aren't you?"

She still can't speak, but Hades doesn't seem to mind. "Aren't you going to finish your desert?" she asks, teasing.

"Aren't you?" Persephone replies, in a voice far more confident than she feels. It makes Hades smirk. She pulls Persephone's hand into her lap and places the pastry on the plate beside them.

"Let's save that for later." Hades pulls Persephone's hand up to her mouth, and Persephone presses her thumb against the plushness of Hades' bottom lip, pink jam smearing across it. Hades takes it in her mouth, slow and deliberate. Never taking her eyes off of Persephone's. She does that with each of Persephone's fingers until they've all been kissed clean.

"All done," she announces.

Persephone shakes her head, a devilish idea crossing her mind. "You still have some." She surges up to push Hades' shoulders so she lays back on the blanket. Persephone swings one leg over her hips, effectively straddling her. But not touching her, not yet. "Right… here." She leans down, hands on either side of Hades' head, and kisses her like it's the only thing she's ever wanted to do in her life. Hades' hands skim along her ribcage, up and down. It warms her and electrifies her. Hades' touch comes to rest at Persephone's hips, pulling them down gently. She allows them to fall, resting her entire weight on Hades. She wills the nagging of insecurity, that she's too heavy, to dissolve. Hades can handle her. She can do more than that. Her muscular thigh presses against the juncture at Persephone's hips with the most delicious pressure. Persephone sighs into the kiss, reveling in her warmth, and her body. Soft where she needs it to be soft and hard where she needs it to be hard. She could lay like this forever, she thinks. Hades has her tongue in her mouth and their breathing is picking up alongside each other's. Persephone grinds down on Hades' thigh, and a quiet moan slips out. Hades bites her lower lip, gentle.

"That might be the most beautiful sound I've ever heard," Hades says. And Persephone blushes, despite their compromising position. It's her words that make her bashful.

"You talk too much."

That makes her laugh. "Oh yeah?"

Persephone nods, with a faux-serious face.

"Well that's too bad," she says. In a second, she's flipped them so Persephone's under her and her hips are nestled between Persephone's legs. One of her forearms is tucked under Persephone's head as a pillow. "Because I have a lot to talk about. I guess you'll just have to be tortured with my too-many words."

Hades buries her face in Persephone's neck, attacking the skin on her throat with open-mouthed kisses and gentle nips. "Beautiful." Kiss. "Μωρό μου."

"What did you say?"

She tuts. "Your mother never taught you the language of home."

"I didn't know the gods spoke a different language."

"We do. We originate in Greece, all the way across the continent from where your mortal village is. And at a different time." She says all this while interspersing her words with attention to Persephone's neck, clavicle, and shoulder.

"A different time."

"Yes, Κούκλα μου. Why your mother chose to hide you in medieval England is beyond me."

"What is medieval?"

"The time period in which you and your mother live. Gods mostly exist out of time."

Her mind feels blown wide open. "You always reveal important information at the worst time."

"My apologies. I just didn't expect you not to know Greek."

"Will you teach me?"

"I'll teach you anything you want to know." Hades is nibbling on her ear now, and she's utterly distracted. Again. "Φως των ματιών μου."

Persephone has no idea what she's saying to her, but with the tenderness the words are spoken, she knows she's praising her, or otherwise showing her some sort of affection. And she soaks it up. She could live off of the low timbre of Hades' voice speaking foreign words into her hair for the rest of her life, she thinks. She pushes her hips into Hades', slightly, just to get that heavenly pressure back for a moment. Hades gets the message and presses her thigh against Persephone's center again. That Persephone could arouse her, one of the most powerful beings to ever exist, is puzzling to her. That she could doubly gain her attachment is another thing altogether.

"Tell me what you're saying," she says.

"No. *I talk too much.*"

She rolls her eyes at Hades' dramatics, but an idea strikes her. She threads her fingers through Hades' hair, scratching lightly at her scalp. It's dark against her fingers, soft and curly. The goddess groans. "Please," Persephone asks. She presses a kiss to her head.

Hades looks up. "Did you just kiss my head?"

Persephone stops playing with her hair, eyes wide. "Yes?" Did she do something wrong?

"No one's ever done that before."

"Really?" How could anyone not shower her in affection?

Hades nods.

"Should I not have done that?"

"No. You should most certainly do that. Over and over again."

Persephone obliges, smattering kisses all over her face. She likes the warmth of Hades' skin beneath her lips and the way she smells this close.

"Fine, fine." Hades pulls away, obviously trying to hide a smile. "I'll tell you what I said. You're very persuasive."

"I'm waiting."

"I said 'my baby.'" Lips on Persephone's cheek. "My doll." Lips on her jaw. "Light of my eyes." Teeth on her neck.

Persephone tugs on her hair lightly. She doesn't want to hurt her, but she likes this edge they're on, these gentle violences they enact upon each other, if violence could ever be called such. The way Hades bites her, soft. She must like having her hair pulled, because she grinds down into Persephone again, setting a rhythm.

"You feel so good," Persephone tells her, shocked at

her own honesty.

"You have no idea how good I can make you feel." She all but growls. It sends a shiver down Persephone's spine and she holds Hades closer to her. The kisses start traveling lower then, below her clavicle and towards her heartbeat. She pulls at the collar of her dress to mouth along the valley between her breasts.

"I think you may be the death of me," Persephone breathes.

"Can I touch you?"

She freezes, because she doesn't know. Touch her where? The idea of it sounds simultaneously horrific and splendid. The last thing she wants and the only thing she wants. Her body aches for it, but it's terrifying. What is wrong with her? She should just nod and be normal. Why can't she be normal? She nods, trying to dislodge what feels like a stone in her throat.

Hades shakes her head. "I don't think so."

"What?"

"If it's a yes it needs to be verbal and without hesitation. I'll touch you when you want it without a second thought."

Persephone's face flushes at how easily she reads her. "I'm sorry."

"Absolutely not. Don't be sorry for anything like that. Would you like us to take a step back or can I move again?"

"Move, please!" she wiggles her hips as she says it, wanting this embarrassment to be over with and for that exquisite friction to begin again.

Hades laughs at her impatience, ducking to kiss her forehead. It's slow, sweet, and with no ulterior motives. Persephone blinks owlishly up at her.

"May I continue kissing your neck?"

"You must."

"Of course, your majesty." Hades' sarcasm has no bite to it, not when she's smiling down at her like that. When

Persephone's sure she can't bear Hades looking at her any longer, she gets back to work and any distressing thoughts are wiped clean from the slate of her mind.

They lay like that for what feels like forever, in perfect harmony with each other, rocking to a rhythm of their own making. The pleasure in her core ratchets up thrust by thrust, amplified by Hades' soft panting in her ear. Her breathing gets heavier and heavier and she covers her mouth with her hand when she's sure she's about to make some humiliating sound, and Hades wrenches it away.

"No. I want to hear you." She punishes Persephone with a particularly hard thrust that draws a moan from her. "There you go, baby. αγαποὐλα μου. Sing for me."

Persephone can barely think. Hades' voice and body fills up her surroundings so thoroughly that all she can do is obey. She rocks her hips into hers and moans again, smiling at the string of praise that falls from her wicked mouth. The seam of Hades' pants brushes against her heat in a very specific way that has her seizing up, hissing "Oh fuck."

Hades grabs her thigh and pulls it up around her waist, making the angle even better than before. "Are you going to come, baby?"

Persephone nods, closing her eyes against the onslaught of what is to come.

"Say it."

She shakes her head. That would be too much.

"Say it. Now." Hades slows her hips on purpose, and Persephone wants to scream at her.

"No, no, no, no." she says, scrambling to pull her back to the previous tempo. "Please. I - I'm going to come."

Hades picks up the pace. "Good. So good for me, ἀγγελέ μου."

It's that last bit of praise that tips Persephone over the edge. Hades holds her close as she buries her face in her shoulder, convulsing, stars filling up her body and exploding pulse by pulse. Something between a growl and a groan escapes Hades and she ruts against her harder than before, hips stuttering. Finally, they slow and eventually still. Persephone's heart is racing. She feels boneless. After a few seconds Hades looks up at her. "Are you okay?"

She nods.

"Are you sure?"

"I'm sure."

Hades rolls them over so she's on her back and Persephone's cuddled against her side, head on her chest. She likes this. She needs this. To be held so she can't fall apart after what just happened. She loved every second of it. She wants to crawl inside of this goddess, seek shelter from herself. From her own desire. They lay there like that for a while, in silence and peace.

Persephone has almost dozed off when she hears Hades curse under her breath.

"What's wrong?" she asks, groggily.

"We have to get back soon."

"Why?"

"If you haven't noticed, princess, you have a very dramatic effect on me. While you have a dress to hide your arousal, I have tight, thin pants. I'm certain I'm soaked through."

Persephone bursts out laughing. "Poor baby."

Hades reaches beside her and throws a pastry at Persephone's head, which bounces off. Persephone's still laughing as she takes a bite of it.

CHAPTER 20

They walk back, Hades insisting that Persephone bundle up in the blanket for the trek and scolding her for not bringing something warm. She doesn't mind it. It's nice to be taken care of, to be fussed over. Hades' gait is off, she notices. Pride blooms in her chest. She made the goddess of the underworld wet. Hades did most of the work, but still. She wonders how many people can say that. Perhaps a few, according to what Hades said about her past. Logically, Persephone knows it's natural for people to have had multiple partners in their lives, but something about it makes her want to cling to Hades like a monkey and glare daggers at anyone who dares come near. She's hers. She doesn't know how long she'll allow herself to be hers, but there's no question about it at the moment.

"You're staring," Hades accuses, not looking up from the glass she's scrubbing. She's changed into clean pants and a loose sleep shirt, and now they're washing the picnic dishes together. She washes, Persephone dries, and tries to find which of the gazillion cabinets they belong to.

"Sorry."

"Do I have something on my face?"

"Yes. It's called ugly."

Hades puts down the glass to stare at her incredulously. Persephone laughs at the expression on her face, and in response she splashes water at her. It's a joke she would've made to Lila at one point.

"You know, not many people would dare say that to my face. You're lucky I like you." She's acting annoyed, but there's a smile creeping at the side of her mouth.

Hades gives Persephone a kiss on the temple when she bids her goodnight. She catches her arm before she can walk away and tugs her back. Hades looks at Persephone, eyes wide, as she places a hand on each side of her face and pulls her down at the same time she goes on her tip-toes. Persephone presses a kiss to her forehead. Solid and lasting. Then she slips into her room. Hades is still standing there, looking at her when she closes the door.

She sinks into the bathtub later that night, body feeling both electrified and exhausted. The first real touch of a woman, and it felt fantastic. The sound Hades made as she came replays in her mind over and over. Persephone can almost still feel her warm breath tickling the baby hairs at the nape of her neck. She hasn't felt this good in a long, long time. So safe, but imperiled beyond belief. Hades will ruin her, she's sure of it. She'll be so kind and dangerous and funny until Persephone becomes irreparably attached to her. Maybe she'll get bored. Maybe she'll find someone that has all the things Persephone lacks and doesn't get upset at simple things and is ready to do anything and everything when she wants it. Maybe she'll demand Persephone go back. Either way, surely she wouldn't keep her forever, no matter how much she wishes she would. But that is an issue for Persephone in the future, she decides. Persephone of the present day can just appreciate what she has before it's gone.

She feels a bit shy the next morning, unsure how to greet Hades at breakfast. Nothing and everything feels different. Persephone is afraid of her and she adores her.

Adores her because she let her get so close and she was careful with her, understanding, and gentle. Afraid of her because it leaves her vulnerable. Hades has Persephone's heart cradled in her hands, like her body was last night. She has the power to crush it or protect it. Persephone hopes to gods she chooses the latter.

With the look in Hades' eyes this morning, one would think Persephone's the one with all the power. She looks at her like she's something precious, something as necessary to her as the sun is to the plants or the moon is to the tides. How odd, Persephone thinks. How preposterous.

They chat about nothing particularly important. How did you sleep? Fine, how about you? Are your legs sore from walking? Yes, not too bad though. The tea is particularly delicious this morning. Yes, I think so too. They play these roles, things unspoken lacing the words they do say. I don't regret last night. You make me so very happy. I'm so glad I found you.

Training is fun. Hades splits their lesson between magic and simple hand-to-hand combat. So she'll always have something to fall back on. And fall she does. Hades tells her to try to tackle her, and shows her the ways in which she can take down someone larger. Aim low. Though Persephone's opponents may be stronger and taller than her like Hades is, not all of them will be as fast. And many of them will certainly underestimate her. She teaches her how to use that to her advantage. Act quickly, feint to the right and then go left, use her teeth if need be. Her favorite part of training, though she doesn't want to admit it to herself, is when she practices defending herself against an oncoming attacker. Hades grabs her from behind, firm but not rough. She has Persephone in a bear hug so she can't use her arms. Persephone goes through the motions as Hades instructs in her ear, but worries she'll hurt her. Stomping on the top of her foot is one thing, but kicking her leg back to her stomach is another. Hades concedes, saying later she'll have someone else practice for real with Persephone if she doesn't think she'll be able to give it her all against her.

"Maybe I'll convince Thanatos to come. You'll love his sunny disposition."

"Who's that?" Persephone asks, miming elbowing her in the ribs.

Hades loosens her hold, miming the shock of the blow. "He's the one that greets people when it's time for them to die. He brings them to me."

"Sounds like the grim reaper."

"The grim reaper sounds like him."

Hades grabs Persephone by the shoulder and she ducks, hooking her leg behind Hades'. Hades falls against the mat. She starts to get up but Persephone puts one foot on her sternum.

"You've been conquered," she informs her.

Hades grins, wrapping her hands around Persephone's ankle. "You're getting cocky." She pulls it to the side, and Persephone has no choice but to fall onto her, straddling her lap.

"Mad because you've been beaten by a novice?" Persephone ignores the fact that she didn't actually defeat her and everything she did was mimed.

"Hardly." Hades flips them over. "In fact, I enjoy it thoroughly." Her hips press into Persephone's so she can feel her heat. Persephone grins up at her, hoping she'll kiss her or, or *something*. Hades shakes her head, rolling her eyes. "Ugh. We're supposed to be training. You're an obnoxious, distracting, little brat." She peppers hisses all over Persephone's face, who giggles at the onslaught. "No more! We have to focus." Hades' voice is stern but her eyes are soft.

"Yes, ma'am." Persephone runs her fingers through Hades' hair.

She narrows his eyes at her. "Stop that."

"Stop what?"

"If you keep misbehaving, we'll get nothing done and I'll have to assign you a new teacher."

Persephone gasps. "You wouldn't."

"I would."

She glares at Hades for a few seconds. "Fine."

Hades gets up and offers her a hand, which she ignores, petulant.

"Are you pouting?"

"No."

"You are."

"Then make me stop." Persephone gets into a defensive stance, ready for whatever attack Hades mounts next.

She lunges.

.

CHAPTER 21

Demeter does not wait long before figuring out that she will have to travel to the underworld herself if she wants to get her daughter back. The meeting in the meadow was an absolute disaster, and she cursed herself and Aetius for letting Persephone slip away. She could almost stand it more if Hades had dragged her away, kicking and screaming. But instead her daughter had gone willingly, looking at her with the saddest eyes she'd ever seen. She wishes she could understand her daughter. Persephone has a tendency to be rash, something that Demeter thought she would grow out of eventually. But perhaps it's just built into her nature. And she doesn't fully believe the prince when he says Persephone stabbed him because his proposal was offensive to her, but she thinks he can help her get her back. He has armies of men at his disposal. Demeter, though a god, is just one woman.

Demeter stands in the meadow where she last saw her daughter, twirling a coin between her fingers. It's been a while since she traveled to any other realm, and she's pretty rusty. But she focuses, fingernails biting into her palms, thinking only of her destination. It's a murky, deadly river. Black sand and fragments of bones line the shore. There's a lone, cloaked figure in a boat, a long pole in his hand. Flickering candles around the edge of the boat, making the shadows twitchy. It will be misty and cold. A cave, yes. It's a cave. She's remembering. She breaks out in a sweat focusing so hard, clenching her fists at her sides.

And then she feels the cool sand beneath her feet. She opens her eyes and exactly what she pictured is in front of her. She smiles. Not too rusty at all, though she likely won't be able to use her power for a day with the amount of effort it took to get here.

"Charon," she calls out. Her voice echoes, bouncing around the dark walls. The cavern around her is huge, with just the smallest ray of sunlight leaking from a crack far above her head.

The figure she imagined is here, and he lifts his head, though the hood of the cloak shrouds his face in shadow.

"It's been a long time," says Charon, voice graveled.

"Take me to him."

"Do you have payment?" Straight to the point. She appreciates it. Iris had tried to chat her ear off.

She walks over and holds out her hand, the gold coin glinting in the candlelight. Why so many godly services require coins, she wishes she knew. Zeus would tell her something about the sanctity of gold, etc. etc. but she never understood. The only gold she sees is of the grain, the kind of gold that will fill bellies.

"Very well," Charon says. He holds out his arm as if welcoming her aboard. She climbs into the boat but doesn't sit. She stands, balanced at the bow. He uses the pole to push off of the shore. She promises herself that on the boat ride back, she'll have Persephone in tow.

CHAPTER 22

Persephone can tell the instant Hades tenses up that something has happened. She has Persephone on the floor as she lays sideways, leaning over her body. Hades' ribs are at Persephone's hip and she's holding himself up with an elbow on her other side. She was talking about how to free oneself should an attacker pin one to the ground, and Persephone was mostly nodding and staring at her as she talked, not really listening. Hades tenses up suddenly, stopping mid-sentence. She stares at the air above Persephone's head.

"Hades?"

"Someone's here."

"What?"

"Someone's here. A god." She rises and helps Persephone up.

"Who? How can you tell?" Persephone follows her as she leaves the training room and walks down the hallway, pace faster than she's seen before. She has to work to keep up.

"I can just sense it. And I think," Hades' frown deepens. "I think it's your mother."

"Oh," She can't help but cringe, though she supposes

she should have expected something like this sooner or later. "Oh, no."

They walk into the throne room and Hades goes straight to sit on her throne, awaiting Demeter's arrival.

"Tari," she says, and the man suddenly appears at her side. Can he shadow-hop too?

"Yes, lord?"

"Will you fetch Persephone's chair please?"

"Yes, lord."

"No, it's okay," she insists. She's so jittery she'd rather pace than have to stay still.

"Are you sure?" Hades asks.

Persephone's mind is running too fast to answer at the moment. She just feels dread, and guilt, and anxiety. She feels as if she might be sick.

"Get it just in case, Tari." Hades then gets back up from her chair. Her palm cradles Persephone's cheek as she looks into her eyes. "Are you okay? What can I do?"

"I think I'm going to be sick."

"Hey, look at me. Look. At. Me."

Persephone does, albeit reluctantly.

"I've got you. Would you like to go somewhere else? You don't have to be here if you don't want to. I can try to...speak to her."

Persephone shakes her head. She knows her mother will just be more enraged if she's not present. "I have to see her. Please don't…egg her on."

Tari comes back with two other staff members behind him, carrying the chair Persephone had sat in at the ball. They set it right beside Hades' throne, bow, and see their way out.

It looks like they are both rulers here. She can't imagine what her mother will think when she sees two thrones, one obviously her daughter's.

The big doors across from them open and before Tari can announce her, Demeter walks in.

Her boots thudding across the floor are the only sound.

Steady, thump, thump, thump. She stops at the bottom of the dais upon which Hades is sat and Persephone is standing. There are bags under her eyes, Persephone notices.

"Persephone," Demeter begins, but her speech peters out as if she doesn't know what to say.

Persephone doesn't respond.

"My love," Demeter says it like it's a plea and a reassurance. "I want to speak with you about the other day."

Persephone waits.

"I'm sorry for the way things went. I just want to talk."

"You'll try to drag me back with you." Persephone's voice shakes.

Demeter takes a deep breath. "I won't be dragging anybody. Please let us talk, just you and me."

Persephone glances back at Hades. For permission or reassurance, Demeter knows not.

"This distance between us is not normal, Seph. I don't want it to be like this," Demeter shakes her head. "You're my little girl. The most important thing in my life."

Persephone looks away. Demeter knows one more word will be enough for her to relent. "Please."

"Okay. We can talk. But you can't try to convince me to come back."

Demeter nods.

Hades rises from her chair, and gently touches Persephone's arm as she leans into her. To an outsider, it may look as if she's pressing a quick kiss to her hair, but Demeter can see her lips moving, and Persephone's minute nod. She makes her way past Demeter without a word and out the doors.

Persephone watches her go, and Demeter catches the wistfulness in her gaze. Her poor, lovesick fool of a girl. She will break your heart, Demeter wants to say. Trust no one who makes a home of the dark. But she knows Persephone will not listen.

"I suppose you should come up here and sit," Persephone says. After a moment's hesitation, she sits on the large throne Hades had been in and Demeter turns the other chair to face it.

"So," Persephone says.

"So."

"How did you want to start?"

"I guess we should start with what happened between you and Aetius. You know what he says happened, yes?"

"Yes." Persephone's face turns white.

"But that is not what you say happened."

"Because it's not."

"So then tell me."

"I," Persephone clears her throat. "I don't know how." And she doesn't want to. It's too much to speak out loud, to put in front of another person. Especially another person who she loves so much and is afraid to lose. Demeter may be a goddess, but at the end of the day she is still just a woman. What if Aetius tried to harm her? Demeter could hold her own most likely, but at what number of men would it be too much for her? Fifty soldiers? One-Hundred? One-thousand? If Demeter believed Persephone she would no doubt go after Aetius and possibly endanger herself. If Demeter doesn't believe Persephone…well, Persephone doesn't want to think about that.

"I can see you thinking," Demeter says. She reaches across the space to smooth out the furrow on her daughter's brow. Persephone's eyes fill with tears at the touch. "You can tell me, you know. Whatever it is."

"I don't think I can, mother. I know I need to, but."

"Did you really stab him?"

"Yes. And strangled him with vines."

Demeter nods, stoic. Not even phased about her daughter using her powers. "And not just over a marriage proposal?"

"Do you honestly think I would have stabbed him over

something as simple as that?"

"Marriage proposals are no simple thing."

"Mother."

"I don't know, love. I don't. I don't know what goes on inside that head of yours. But I'm not mad at you for stabbing him, whatever he did. I just don't understand why you ran away."

Persephone snaps her head up. "They were chasing me. With blades and torches. I had no choice."

Demeter leans forward. "You could have found a place to hide in the woods, waited for me to come home and find you. You didn't have to leave the mortal realm completely."

"And where was I to hide that they couldn't find me? How long would I have been stuck in those woods until you came home? How would you even have known where to look?"

"That was safer than running off with a woman you barely know! And a God at that! How did you even run into her?"

Persephone can feel her face getting red.

"I told you, I don't really know how or why it happened. I-I had a dream about her."

"You what?"

"I saw her in a dream and in that dream she gave me a seed. And when I was running away from those men, I fell, and something happened and the seed was right beside me. I made it grow, mother. With my own power. And then Hades arrived." Persephone fiddles with her thumbs. "I think I summoned her that way, though I didn't know it at the time."

"That makes no sense."

"I don't know what to tell you. It's the truth."

"And what? She just offered to bring you down to the underworld oh-so-benevolently and you jumped in her arms?"

Persephone sits back, fury flaring in her chest. "Don't

speak to me like that."

Demeter shakes her head and closes her eyes. "I'm sorry. You're right. I'm just frustrated, Persephone."

"You care about that more than Aetius, don't you?"

"I care about it more because gods can hurt you in ways mortals can't. I don't want you to go through what I went through, my love. Ever."

"What did you go through? You never told me! You always deflected and griped but you never once told me the truth of what happened. And I tried to stop asking after a while, like a good daughter, and look where it got me. All of that secrecy led to this."

Demeter's mouth forms a tight line. "Fine. I'll tell you."

Persephone leans forward.

"But you must promise me that after I tell you, you will go home with me."

"You said you wouldn't try to drag me back with you!"

"I said I wouldn't drag you. This would mean you'd go willingly with me."

"You lied to me."

"You wouldn't have spoken to me otherwise, and I didn't technically lie. You told me not to ask you about coming back, and I nodded."

Persephone scoffs.

"Do you want to know or not?"

Persephone is silent for a moment and then sighs. She can play this game. Hell, she ought to be an expert with a teacher like Demeter. "If you tell me what happened, I will go home."

Demeter's shoulders sag, as if she's let go of a huge weight on her shoulders. "Thank you, dear. Thank you."

"Go ahead."

Demeter explains about her eons in the celestial family. About the lies and the affairs and the broken trust among all of them, all of the time. About how Zeus had seduced her to his bed with the explanation that his wife Hera knew he took other lovers and was with her own lover at that moment. Demeter, in her lust and desire to be desired, believed him. A few months later, her belly began getting rounder. How delighted she was to have a partner in this world. And then Hera came to her, red hot with betrayal and spitting ugly words that could never be taken back. She had known Zeus was unfaithful but hated it. And hated Demeter for enabling him. She wasn't with her own lover after all. Demeter tried to apologize but with godly powers comes godly emotions, and the fury of it all was too much for Hera to shake. Zeus had simply shrugged when Demeter tried to confront him about it, with that lazy smile of his. That smile that said he'd always gotten what he wanted, and always will, no matter the cost to other people. When she'd told him she was pregnant, he simply laughed. Better not let Hera know, he said. She'll try to kill you and it. Demeter had launched herself at him, trying to claw that stupid smile off of his face and he had sparked lightning at her, electrified her very bones and threw her yards away. The heartbreak and concern for the little one growing in her stomach was too much. She fled the celestial sphere and never looked back, determined to never be like them.

"You're not telling me everything," Persephone accused. She could always tell, with her mother. When she didn't want to tell the whole story. It's happened Persephone's whole life.

Demeter swallowed. "That's what happened."

"That's not all that happened though. I know you, mother."

"I swear that's all," Demeter rises from the seat. "Now it's time to go."

"Is it?" Persephone asks.

"Yes. You now know the whole wretched tale. Let's go home now."

Persephone just looks at her mother. "You aren't telling me everything, and I'm not going."

"Persephone. Get up this instant."

"No, I won't.

Demeter narrows her eyes. "You accused me of lying, and now look at you."

"I didn't promise I'd go with you immediately after you spoke. I just said I'd come home, which could be at any time."

Demeter reaches for Persephone, not aggressively, but Persephone has had enough. She yells, "Hades!"

She's by her side in an instant.

Demeter takes a step back. "I never thought I'd see the day where we would be on opposite sides."

"Does that mean you'll take Aetius's side?"

"No, love. I'm not that cruel. But I won't let you stay here forever. I will fight to get you back."

"I know," Persephone says, tears brimming. Tears of frustration, tears of devastation.

"I love you more than life itself, you know that, don't you?"

"I do know. But it's not always in the way I need you to."

"You'll have to face him sooner or later," Demeter says. "He'll tear the world apart looking for you."

"I will face him."

Demeter looks off into the distance for a moment. "He will go after Lila."

"What?"

"He said he would go after her if you hadn't appeared within a month. That was a week ago, so you now have three weeks left to face him."

"Why didn't you tell me this at the beginning?" Persephone demands, panic seizing her chest.

"I thought I could get you to come back with me today, and then you wouldn't have to worry about it."

Persephone scrambles to think. Of course Aetius would do this. "You can protect her, can't you?"

Demeter looks at her daughter with something like sadness in her eyes, something like an apology.

Persephone takes a step backward. "You won't do it. You won't protect her, on purpose, so that I'll come up. You'd be willing to let her die"

Demeter doesn't respond. Persephone's shoulders heave, on the verge of hyperventilation. Hades lays a hand at the small of her back.

"I think it's time for you to go," Hades says to Demeter. Her voice helps ground Persephone a bit.

"Go," Persephone says. When her mother doesn't make a move she yells, "GO!"

"I love you, dear," Demeter says, and it's genuine. But it's not enough. She turns and walks to the door. Palm on the handle, she looks back at her daughter as if waiting for her to say 'nevermind.'

But Persephone doesn't say that. Instead, she says "You are *exactly* like them."

Something like pain crosses over her mother's face, barely-there flinch that she's never seen her mother do before. Demeter slips through the door, and the small child in Persephone wants to run after her and beg forgiveness, but the adult hopes that she feels all of the hurt that Persephone feels. Once her mother is out of sight, she lets out a sob. There is so much going on inside her that it's hard to breathe, hard to think. She covers her mouth wishing she could shove it back in. Wishing she could be strong and stoic and confident, but she's none of those. She doesn't know where she's inherited this weakness from.

"Hey, hey, hey," Hades speaks softly to her, stroking her hair. "It's alright."

"No, it's not!" she wails. "Nothing is alright!" She feels her legs itching to go, to run. She can't stay still. But the last time she ran out of the castle she was attacked by that...thing. Maybe that's what she needs. To tear into something.

"I've got to go," she tells Hades. "That thing that attacked me last time, there are more like it, right?"

153

"Yes, but I've made sure they won't come near here anymore."

"Can you undo that?"

She looks at her, brow furrowed. "Yes...why?"

CHAPTER 23

And that's how Persephone ends up sprinting past the edge of the garden, fidgety as she waits for the beasts to arrive. Hades had told her to be careful after she let down the magic that safeguarded the gardens. Looked her seriously in her eyes and made her swear to call if she needed help. She agreed, grateful that Hades understood her need to be alone. But she wouldn't call for her.

These things feed on anger, grief, and fear. She will give them all of those.

She stalks deeper into the forest, purposefully stepping on twigs and leaves, listening intently. Shadows dart around the edges of her vision, some perhaps the size of a bunny and others...far bigger. And she welcomes it. She welcomes those shadows, that darkness. She welcomes it to her and into her.

She's almost to the base of the mountain upon which she and Hades had their date, when she finally gets the telltale prickling on the back of her neck. The hairs on her arms and legs stand up and the air gets colder, so cold that her breath comes out in white clouds. She acts like she doesn't know it's watching her and continues walking.

It follows. She doesn't know how she knows, but she does. She can just feel it. The ground and air around her is electric with the tension. She imagines curling her power around her fist like the ends of a rope, or whip. It rises to meet her thoughts.

"Come and get me," she whispers. A low snarl rips through the forest behind her and suddenly there are barbs digging in her shoulders. She twirls around, cursing herself for not acting before it cut her, but in a way the pain is a relief. There is only her and this beast, nothing more and nothing less. She uses a pulse of her power to blow it back, not even thinking about using plants. She tucks that away for later, to ask Hades about. The thing crouches, its limbs digging into the earth. It's just as terrifying as she remembers. At this moment it wears Aetius's face, and her own splits into a grin. It roars at her and she, all 5'8 of her, roars back. The scream scratches her throat but gods, it feels so good to make so much noise. It crawls at her, quick as lightning, spindly legs bending at every joint.

Just as it's about to tackle her, she dodges and leaps onto its back, wrapping her arms around its stretched neck as tight as she can. It squeals and rears up, then falls backwards so she's pinned beneath it.

It knocks the breath out of her. It's not a very heavy creature, but it's a shock. She wraps her legs around its round abdomen, which turns out to be a bad idea. Two of its legs grab her ankle and nearly pulls her leg out of its socket.

"Shit!" she hisses, and has to let go of it completely so as not to be ripped apart. It rolls over so she's off its back and in the dirt beside it. It drags her toward it as she kicks and grunts. It opens its pincers wide, showing needle-sharp fangs webbed with spittle and roars again, in her face this time.

And, of course, she roars back. It lunges to bite into her shoulder but she rolls out of the way at the last second and kicks in the jaw.

It shakes its head, a small whine coming out. It pauses for a second, and then its face morphs into her mother's. She expected this. But it doesn't mean that she doesn't hesitate before kicking the limbs that hold her leg with all her might. That split second of hesitancy costs her. Its fangs sink into her left shoulder and she bites her bottom lip to keep from screaming. It stings like nothing she's ever felt before. Blood begins pouring out of the wound and it hasn't even let go yet. But she knows Hades is probably waiting to hear her scream and will run to her rescue as soon as she does, and she doesn't want that. She needs the gritty feeling of handling this beast on her own, preferably with her bare hands for as long as she possibly can.

She kicks and claws and bucks but it only digs its fangs deeper into her shoulder. She should call the roots below to drag it off of her, dig into its eyes or mouth until it lets go, but she doesn't want to. So she does the only other thing she can think of, and bites it back. She aims for the flesh of its neck, right beside her face. It makes a noise, something akin to surprise, and she can feel its fangs loosen a fraction. Though its black blood is acrid on her tongue and its skin cold and clammy beneath her lips she bites down as hard as she can. Finally the thing lets go of her shoulder. But she won't let it pull away. It scrambles to remove her but she holds on tight, and right as one large, barbed leg swings toward the skin of her side, she tears away from it, the piece of flesh still between her teeth.

It lets out an ungodly shriek, crawling backwards away from her, stumbling. Now that its face is not buried in her shoulder she sees her mother's face on its own again. It pants, the fangs too large to let its mouth close, and its nostrils flare with each sharp inhale. She stares back at it, spitting out the piece of flesh on the ground between them. And the look it gives her - a look she's never seen her mother have before - it's fear. A pit grows in her stomach. She knows logically that this thing is not her mother, that it's using her own emotions against her, but she can't help it. She wants to weep for the guilt washing over her.

And somehow, it can tell. Perhaps her guilt has a smell. Perhaps these creatures are just very adept at reading human emotion. Her shoulders sag and she exhales. She isn't sure she wants to fight this thing anymore. She takes a step back without taking her eyes off it, hoping it will understand. It gets the message. The message that its opponent is emotionally and physically weakened, and it takes a step towards her.

"No," she says. "That's over."

She takes another step backwards, which it follows with another step forward. The look on its face, her mother's face, is neutral.

"Oh," she says. It had never been afraid of her at all. And that makes her so, so angry.

Before she even realizes it, she's running at it with all her might and it leaps at her and they land on the forest floor with a thud, a tangle of claws and teeth and grunts and pure hatred. Both of them. It gets a swipe down her cheek. She gets a kick on its side. It snaps at her neck and she misses a swing to its abdomen. It roars in her face, spittle flying between them. She roars back, and a second too late realizes the creature wanted her to do that. It shoves the end of a limb into her mouth, hooked on the inside of her jaw as if it would rip it clean off. It all becomes very clear for her at that moment. When it tries to pull down, she doesn't resist. And then she bites the end clean off. She had heard when she was younger that one can bite through their own finger as easily as a carrot, but it's just the instinct of the mind that makes it impossible.

The creature's limb does not snap as easily as a carrot, but it goes easier than she thought it would. It screams and screams and rips itself away from her, scrambling backwards. The claw falls out of her mouth, a gnarled gray thing. She follows it. And tackles it with her entire body to the ground. It thrashes and growls, but she manages to pin it beneath her knees so all it can do is kick and buck. She pays that no mind. It snaps its pincers in the air and its face twitches, morphing before her eyes into Lila. It's a face she hasn't seen in a long time. She stares down at it while it wiggles, trying to be free of her. The hazel-green of her old friend's eyes and the brown curls and the freckles over the bridge of her nose. The creature hisses lowly, and Persephone is brought back to reality. It's odd, she thinks. She doesn't fear Lila. Maybe this is a last-ditch effort of the creature to extort a different emotion of hers than fear, to spare its life? She doesn't know and she doesn't want to think about it. She wraps her hands around its neck and squeezes. It's not really Lila. It's not really Lila. It's just a creature that feeds off your emotions. If you don't kill it, it will torture some other soul. It's okay. It's okay. It's okay. Tears stream down her face and she feels the urge to vomit. She can't even kill normal-sized spiders. Why did she think she could do this? She can't do this. She'll have to use her power to kill it, like last time. It's different with magic. She can't kill something with her bare hands. While she's berating herself and trying to decide what to do, the sputtering of the creature goes quiet and its limbs stop their frantic struggle. She sits there for a moment longer, never letting up the pressure on its throat. There's nothing but the sound of her own ragged breath. She releases the thing finally, and opens her eyes. Its face has returned to its natural state thankfully, a mostly blank stretch of skin with a slit where the mouth is, two small holes for the nose, and huge, bottomless black pits for eyes. She scrambles to get off of it, something about it being dead making her want to wash her whole body for touching it.

She throws up until nothing comes up but acid, wipes her mouth, and begins the walk back towards the castle. She's shaking and startled at the breaking of twigs every once in a while, but it's just the usual creatures that one would see in a forest, in the mortal realm. Something that looks like a fluffy fox that chatters to itself in a foreign language as it passes. A rabbit-looking creature with three eyes. Little toadstools that stood still on her way into the forest are up and walking around. The forest is coming alive again.

CHAPTER 24

Persephone finds Hades pacing in the garden. When she sees Persephone her face breaks into relief, and quickly back into concern.

"What happened? How badly are you hurt?" she asks, holding her at arm's length so she can look her up and down.

"I'm fine," Persephone says. And she is, she thinks. The bite in her shoulder has faded into a dull, pulsing ache and the cuts on her face just feel cold in the wind. The puncture wounds on her leg feel the same as the last time the creature clawed her leg. She knows she must look a wreck though.

"You're bleeding all over the place!" Hades fusses, her thumb probing gently at the slices on Persephone's cheek. Then her eyes travel down to her shoulder and widen. "Were you *bitten*?"

"Not too bad."

"*Persephone.*"

"It doesn't even hurt that much anymore," she mumbles.

"They're venomous!" Hades runs a hand through her hair, and Persephone feels a bit bad for causing her so much stress. And how dangerous can the venom be if she only feels a bit sluggish? "Come on, we have to patch you up before it sets in."

Hades grabs her hand and the earth beneath her seems to fall away. Hades jumps through the shadows rather than walk through the castle. The sudden change makes Persephone sway, and Hades catches her.

"I'm such an idiot," she hears Hades mutter under her breath.

"You're not an idiot," Persephone says. "Why would you say that?" She rights herself and sees that they're in a large bathroom similar to her own, but larger and darker. Everything she can see is made of what looks to be onyx. Candles line the windowsill and basin and shelves. The tub is on a pedestal in the very center of the room, with a flickering chandelier hanging over it.

"I shouldn't have let you go out there alone." Hades leads her over to the counter and grabs her hips, lifting her onto it. While Persephone sits, swinging her feet, she gathers supplies from the various cabinets.

"I wanted to."

"I know. It doesn't mean you should have."

"I'm alive aren't I?"

Hades gives her a look that she knows means something along the lines of 'barely' or 'keep misbehaving and see what happens.'

"I understand you need to get your frustration out, but not at the expense of your safety. You should have yelled for me the second you were injured."

"You expected me to do that, didn't you? You thought I'd cry for you after less than a minute out there?" Her words slur at the edges and a queer numbness begins taking hold of her shoulder.

"No, I expected you to value your safety more than you do." Hades quietly rips the neckline of her dress so she can see her shoulder. She hisses through her teeth when she sees the mark.

"Hey, I liked this dress."

"Sweetheart, you'll have to get in the tub. I can't clean this here." Her words are controlled but Persephone can tell, even through the haziness, there's a tinge of panic in her voice.

"I'll get your fancy tub dirty!"

"That's what it's for." Hades leaves her on the counter for a moment to get the water going, and comes back to help her off the counter. "Down you go."

Persephone's legs feel like jelly and she clutches to Hades like a lifeline, which, she figures, she is in a way. "Strange venom," she mutters. "I just feel a little…dizzy. Or drunk."

"The goal is to incapacitate their prey," Hades says, scooping Persephone up in her arms when she can't make it two feet without stumbling. The movement makes Persephone feel a little nauseous, but she's distracted when Hades sets her in the warm water. "Make them loopy and complacent so they can't fight back."

"My dress is still on," she says.

"This may hurt a bit, baby." Hades is not listening to her. When Persephone tries to turn her head to look at the bite, Hades gently turns her head away. It must be worse than she thought. "So tell me what happened."

"Well it tried to kill me, which is what I wanted it to do because then I could fight it of course." Hades begins to work on cleaning the wound while she speaks, and she watches her move out of the corner of her eye.

"Of course. Can you not feel this?"

"No. It's numb."

Hades sucks in a breath, and then bids her to continue her story.

"It had *his* face at first so it was easy at the beginning. Then it had hers. And it was not so easy."

"I'm sorry." Persephone sees her wet the washcloth and put some sort of soap or ointment on it, and then she brings it to her shoulder. She's listening to her now, though. Persephone can tell by the furrow in her brow and the way she glances at her face every once in a while.

"Then it had Lila's. And I think I snapped."

"You killed it?"

"Yes. At one point I threw it back, not with my hands but with my power. I didn't have to use any plants though. It's like I blew it away with the air or something."

"That's amazing, love."

"I thought so too." She draws her knees up and rests her chin on top of them. The water is still running, up to her waist now. She's so warm and cozy she could fall asleep where she sits. Her eyes begin to close.

"Stay with me, baby," Hades says.

"I'm awake."

"Barely. Come on, talk to me. How did you kill it?"

"I choked it to death." The words coming out of her mouth sound foreign, but after a second she realizes they're true. And a weight starts building in her stomach. She killed something. And yes, she's killed one of those creatures before - but it had attacked her unprovoked. She sought out this one, specifically to have something to fight. No - to kill. She went out there with the intent to kill. "Oh no," she moans, and digs her palms into her closed eyes. "Oh, no no no."

"What's wrong?"

"I killed it!"

"Why are you upset about that?"

"Because it was in pain and I killed it and I didn't even have to!" Tears start streaming out of her eyes and her shoulders shake. Gods, she's a mess.

"Oh, my sweet girl," Hades sighs.

"I'm serious!"

"I know."

After a minute or two of silence in which Persephone stares at the water turning pinker with the blood from her various injuries, Hades speaks again. "It's okay. They're vicious creatures, and you got some practice."

"Why don't you get rid of them?"

"They're part of the ecosystem. And useful for torturing rapists and murderers. Most of the other beings that live down here, like you and me, know how to evade them."

"I think I'm a bad person."

"Bad people don't worry about being bad people."

Persephone isn't certain that's true. "I'm sorry I keep getting injured. You don't have to take care of me."

"I do," she says. "And I do it gladly. I'll take care of you for as long as you let me." She motions for her to lean back. "Drink this. It'll keep the fever down."

Persephone does as she is bid, though her hand shakes as she holds the cup. It's a cool, bittersweet liquid the color of grass. "Bleh."

"I'm done cleaning your shoulder. Where else are you injured?"

She shrugs. "I can do the rest."

"Would you prefer to?"

She shakes her head.

"Then where?"

She lifts her leg up so her ankle rests on the lip of the tub. "Just scratches, like last time."

"These are deeper, though."

When Hades cleans those out, Persephone feels everything. She clenches her jaw and squeezes her fists to keep from reacting to the stinging, but it's over soon. Hades applies the same purple gel she did last time and sets her leg gently back down into the tub.

"Okay, now look at me."

Persephone turns her face towards her, resting her chin on the lip of the tub. Hades' fingers run along the scratch on Persephone's face, then she repeats the same stinging cool process that she did with the cuts on her legs. Persephone revels in her careful, gentle touches. She's almost disappointed when she runs out of injuries for her to tend to.

"You're filthy, darling," Hades says. Persephone cracks one eye open. "You need a bath."

"I'll do my best."

She seems to hesitate a moment, then asks, "Do you need help? Genuinely?"

The numbness in Persephone's shoulder has started to fade and slowly be replaced with a dull aching sensation that gets worse by the minute. She tries to lift her arm but doesn't get very far before the pain is unbearable. She nods, blushing. "I'm sorry."

"Don't be sorry. Would you like me to get Sophia to help you?"

"No. I want you." She's surprised she said it, but she means it wholeheartedly. She can't stand the thought of her leaving right now.

She blinks at her. "You're sure?"

Persephone nods again, "If you're okay with it?"

"I am."

"Could I - I'd like to keep my undergarments on please."

"Of course. Can you stand?"

"I think."

Hades pulls the plug to let the bloody water out and start a new bath. Then she hooks her arms under Persephone's armpits to help her stand. "I'm going to take your dress off now."

"Okay."

She wraps one arm around Persephone's waist to keep her stable and with the other hand pulls the hem of her dress up from her ankles over her hips and ribs. Persephone winces something fierce when she tries to raise her arm so Hades guides it back down and tries to peel the neckline down instead. Thanks to the rip she had made in it earlier, it slides down Persephone's body and lands in the bottom of the tub with a wet plop. She's left standing in her pale pink shift that only goes about midway down her thigh, and sticks to her wet body. Hades guides her back into a seated position and throws the dress to the side. She curls in on herself again, closing her eyes as Hades putters around, throwing things into the steaming water that's rising and getting various soaps. She opens her eyes to find lavender petals floating on the water and some sort of shimmery oil permeating the water.

"This is fancy," Persephone says.

"Tilt your head up," Hades replies, holding the base of Persephone's skull in her palm. She scoops some of the water in a pitcher and pours it over her hair. Persephone is lulled into a sort of stupor by her ministrations, perhaps in part due to the venom but perhaps because she has unlocked an intrinsic part of her that hasn't been fed in a very, very long time. The part of her that just wants to be told what to do and when, that wants someone to take care of her, that needs to be able to totally trust someone with her body and mind. She feels a little like a ragdoll as Hades lathers the length of her arm with a sponge, gathers water in her palm, and wipes the suds away from her skin. It has the perfect amount of coarseness on the part of her back that's exposed. Hades lifts each of her legs and scrubs them gently, up to the hem of her slip. She avoids all parts of her covered by the cloth, never letting her hands linger for too long on one part of her skin. Persephone wouldn't mind if she did, though. She is thankfully able to keep that thought to herself.

After Persephone's body has been washed, Hades takes off her own boots and socks, rolls up the bottom of her trousers, and sits on the edge of the tub behind Persephone, legs in the tub on either side of her. Persephone wants to lean against the side of her knee but she leans her back up. She has no time to grumble, though. She thought it had felt nice when Hades ran the sponge over her skin, but the real ecstasy comes when she lathers her hair, fingertips digging into her scalp just the right amount. She can't help but let out a moan. She hears Hades' intake of breath through her nose.

"I take it that feels good?"

"Mm-hmm." Persephone's been momentarily robbed for words. Hades massages her scalp for a minute or two more despite the shampoo being already lathered. She rinses it out thoroughly with the pitcher.

"Ready to get out?"

Persephone nods and she helps her stand again, wrapping her in a huge, black fuzzy towel.

"Thank you for your help," she says, swaying where she stands.

"You're welcome, love." Hades scoops her up in her arms and walks out of the bathroom, into another dark room. The roaring fire in the large hearth casts flickering light over the place, revealing a canopy bed fitted with black, velvet coverings, an ebony desk and chair, and two armchairs upon a fluffy, burgundy rug, with a small, low table between them.

"This is your room?"

"Yes. Don't worry, I'll take you back to yours."

"That seems like a long way away."

"It's just down the hall. But I need to keep an eye on you while you sleep, in case the fever starts up again."

"Your bed looks very comfortable."

Hades stops walking, partway to the door. "You want to stay here?"

"Yes, please. If that's okay with you."

She nods and Persephone reaches up to trace the curve of her neck as she swallows. She carries her over to the bed and sets her down gently. Persephone misses her warmth instantly.

"I'll have to go get your nightclothes." Hades turns back to the door, but she grabs her hand.

"Don't go, please." If she were in her right mind, she would be embarrassed by her neediness. But she can't find whatever impulse to feel shame that usually infects her. She wraps the towel tighter around her but without the steam of the bathroom, cold seeps in quickly.

Hades looks at where Persephone's hand grips hers. "Okay," she says, as if she's speaking to herself. "Okay." She walks over to a door beside the hearth, and in the split second she disappears into the dark space beyond, Persephone fears she left anyway, but she comes back out with something folded in her arms. It's just a closet. And she's brought Persephone one of her shirts. It's dark blue and made of thick, woven fabric - something akin to a sweater.

"Can you put it on yourself?" He asks, standing in front of where she sits on the bed.

Her words float in and out of her awareness and she only replies, "You're so tall."

"Persephone."

"What?"

Hades shakes her head. "I'm going to put this on you, and you can take off the shift underneath, okay?"

"Okay."

She slips it over her head and kneels in front of her. She looks resolutely off to the side as she helps her maneuver her arms out of the shift beneath, and down over her hips and legs. Persephone still has on undergarments, though - and they're wet and cold. Hades brings out a pair of loose shorts that probably fall around her upper-thigh.

"Are these your undergarments?" Persephone asks.

"Well, you won't let me leave to get yours. And I'm sure you don't want to sleep in the ones you have on."

"I'm sorry."

"No, don't-" Hades sighs. "Don't apologize. I'm not frustrated with you, I promise. I'm going to take those off of you, okay? But I'm not looking."

It's a very embarrassing ordeal to shimmy out of her undergarments and shimmy into another's, but she's grateful once she has the dry, clean ones on. They're so very light and airy.

"These feel amazing," she says. "I think I'll keep

them."

Hades shakes her head, just the corner of her mouth ticking up. She peels back the heavy blanket on the bed and motions for Persephone to lay back.

"Why do you try to hide your smile?" Persephone asks, snuggling deep under the covers.

"I don't." Hades busies herself with putting the wet clothes in the laundry basket.

"You do. You shouldn't, though." She watches her putter around the room. "It's so pretty."

"Pretty." Her back is to Persephone, throwing a log into the already large fire.

"Mm-hmm." Persephone frowns. "Are you coming to bed?"

"I can't sleep, I need to watch you."

"So you're going to stand all night?"

"Well, no. I was going to sit in one of the chairs."

"Why would you do that?" She tries to sit up, frowning.

Hades comes over and gently pushes her shoulder back down. "I didn't want to assume anything. I don't want to make you uncomfortable."

"You're a very kind person."

She tilts her head and opens her mouth to say something that is no doubt irrelevant to what Persephone wants right now, which is Hades, beside her. If she could tackle her, she would in a heartbeat.

"Will you please stop talking and get in bed?"

One of her eyebrows quirk up and Persephone gets the distinct feeling she shouldn't have said that. "You get one little bite from a monster and suddenly think you run this place." Hades' words are soft. Amused. She cups Persephone's cheek in her palm as she kneels by the bed.

"Your hair looks so silky," Persephone informs her, and reaches up to run her fingers through it. It's even silkier than it looks, she finds. But it reminds her – she shoots up in bed, nearly head-butting Hades.

"I have to brush my hair or it will be a nightmare in the morning!"

"Okay, okay. Calm down." Hades rises. "I'll grab a comb." Persephone hears her rustle around in the bathroom for a minute and she returns triumphant, silver-plated brush in one hand.

"Move up." She pushes Persephone's hips away from the headboard and climbs in behind her. She begins brushing through the wet tangles with the same gentleness she had washed her with. It almost feels as nice as when she'd lathered the soap in her hair. Persephone leans her head back as she instructs and closes her eyes, perfectly content.

"Thank you, Hades."

She presses a kiss to the crown of Persephone's head. "Anything for you, princess."

When Hades is done Persephone snuggles down back under the heavy blankets. She lays on her side, facing her goddess as she crawls in. She'd donned loose, black trousers but didn't put on a shirt over her bandeau. Even in Persephone's subdued state, her heart skips a beat. She stares at the plain of Hades' chest above the fabric, the subtle muscle of her stomach underneath a healthy pad of fat and all the curves of her body. She's just so solid.

"Whoa," Persephone says, not really meant for Hades to hear but not caring that much either.

She stops, one knee on the mattress. "What's wrong?"

"Nothing. You're just beautiful."

Her face grows the slightest bit pink, along with the tips of her ears peeking out of her hair. Persephone can't help but grin at her.

"Wow," Hades gets in bed finally and lays on her back, looking up at the black, silk canopy. "Pretty and beautiful, and all in one night? If you wanted to get me in bed so badly you could've just said."

"Did I embarrass you?"

She turns her face to look at Persephone, eyes

narrowed. "Hush and go to sleep."

Persephone's so happy that she doesn't really notice the aching in her shoulder. And she knows, through the haze, that it's the venom making her feel this way. She still has her mother to worry about, and Lila and Aetius and all the rest. But she will take her happiness wherever she can get it, and right now, it's with Hades.

.

CHAPTER 25

She wakes up sometime in the night, hungry and in pain. The venom seems to have completely worn off, and her shoulder pulses. Hades had wrapped a bandage around it so she can't see the damage, but she knows it's bad. Something heavy and warm lays across her waist. She reaches down to feel that it's Hades' arm. They fell asleep facing each other, and sometime after that Hades must've thrown it around her. Persephone's facing her chest, head tucked beneath her chin. Hades' breath tickles the loose hair on top of her head. She moves, lifting her arm slowly so as not to wake her. But even asleep, Hades has strength to be reckoned with. She grumbles in her sleep and tightens her hold on Persephone, drawing her closer. Persephone's face smushes against Hades' chest. She sighs.

"Hades," she whispers. Hades does not react. "Hades!" this time it's louder, and she twitches. Persephone pokes her shoulder - hard. "HADES."

She jerks awake, instinctively squeezing her tighter. "What? What's wrong?"

"I need to get up."

"Oh." She loosens her grip. "How are you feeling?"

"Horrible. I'm going to go get some food."

"I'll go with you." She gets up, wiping a hand down her handsome face. Her hair is adorably mussed from sleep.

"You don't have to."

"I am."

Persephone gets out of bed and her eyes widen when she realizes what she's wearing, and what she's not wearing. "Do you have a robe or something I could borrow?"

"What? You don't want to traipse through the castle in my underwear?"

"I don't traipse," she grumbles.

Hades laughs, voice still husky from sleep. She fetches Persephone a fluffy robe that she says Persephone can keep. It's so snuggly that she feels like she's bringing the bed with her.

She follows Hades down the chilly, dark corridors. She doesn't know who dims the torches at night or if they do that on their own, but it's times like this when she remembers that she's been living in a castle in the *underworld*. But as cold and shadowy as it is, there is still an element of coziness to it. Of home. Maybe it's the vibrant tapestries or the smell of baking bread that wafts up from the kitchen through the stairwells and corridors, or just the knowledge that there are many other people who dwell there.

Hades tries to get her to sit down when they get to the kitchens, but she doesn't want to rest right now. She is fully capable of getting her own food and will prove it.

"*You* sit down," she mutters.

"I'll do no such thing."

"Then hush or make yourself useful."

"You're grumpy," Hades muses. "Does your shoulder hurt?"

Persephone pauses in the middle of slicing cheese for her sandwich. "Yes."

"I'll put more salve on it when we get back. Ham or turkey?"

Persephone glances behind her to see Hades bent over in the pantry, looking through the ice chest. As grumpy as she is, she still appreciates the curve of her ass.

"Ham."

Hades grabs it and straightens up. She catches Persephone staring when she turns around. Persephone looks her up and down, her tall, thick statue of a woman, and slowly turns back to the cheese.

"Something on my face?" Hades comes up beside her and sets down the ingredients she gathered.

"Yes."

Her hand comes up to her cheek. "Where?"

Persephone stands on her tiptoes and inspects her skin closely, then presses a quick kiss on his cheekbone. "There."

Pink crawls into her face and the tips of her ears, again. Persephone likes making that happen. Making her flustered.

After a second she seems to recover and says, "I think you have something on your face too."

"I know I do," Persephone replies, tapping her cheek. "It's right there."

Hades shakes her head, at Persephone's attitude or audacity she knows not which, but she's smiling. She leans down to press a long, soft kiss to the place Persephone indicated. And then another. And another.

Persephone leans away at the fifth kiss, laughing. "I'm trying to make a sandwich."

"You should have thought about that before staring at my ass."

That makes her laugh harder, and with her head thrown back Hades attacks her neck with kisses. She tries to wrap her arms around Persephone but accidentally bumps her shoulder. She hisses at the pain and Hades pulls back completely.

"Sorry, baby," she says, looking guiltier than Persephone's ever seen her.

"It's okay. I think I'll have you make this for me after all." The pain radiates down her arm and she doesn't want to move it anymore until she gets the salve. Hades nods and takes over the process, even toasting the bread and melting the cheese. She brews some tea for them both. They go back up to her rooms to eat, sitting in front of the fireplace. Persephone elects to sit on the rug directly in front of it instead of the chair, just to feel the heat on her face. Hades follows her down without comment and she gets the distinct feeling that Hades would follow her into the pits of Tartarus and back, if she so wished. It's a fuzzy feeling. One that makes her want to cry. She does cry a little, later on when Hades smooths the salve over her wound. But it numbs quickly with every dab of the medicine and every kiss on the head.

The next day they train in the garden at the back of the castle. Various other castle residents lounge about on the grounds outside, soaking up the sun. One little centaur's nose and cheeks turn pinker and pinker in the sun, and what Persephone assumes are his parents or guardians insist he come inside, despite his crying. The day is actually warm. It's the first warm day in the underworld she's ever experienced.

"You did this, you know." Hades says. They are taking a break, sitting under one of the trees farther away from everyone else. "You gave this to them, whether you realized it or not."

"I still don't know how I could've."

"Well you did. You brought us the sun."

She grows a little dandelion from the ground between them. Round and yellow and puffy. It doesn't take as much energy for her to do now, it comes easily. The sun is another matter altogether.

"I hope you don't mind, but I invited Minthe for the

rest of our training today," Hades says, watching some young dryads play pretend with wooden swords.

"I don't mind. Will you be leaving, then?"

"I'll be watching. I just figured that you'd be more likely to unleash your power if it wasn't against me."

"That's probably true."

Minthe arrives in tight trousers and a short-sleeved blouse, barefoot.

"I haven't seen you in a while," she says to Persephone. "Are you ready to fight?"

"Yes," Persephone replies. And she *is* ready to fight, and the fact that Minthe seems to have more of her insufferable swagger this morning helps.

She gets up and faces Minthe in the defensive stance, ready for a kick or a punch, but instead the air whips around her ankles, toppling her to the ground.

"What the hell?" She scrambles to her feet and stares at Minthe, incredulous.

"You didn't think this would be hand-to-hand, did you sweetheart?"

"I didn't know you had powers!"

"You want to touch all over me, I get it. Sorry to disappoint."

"You should have told me before we started!"

"Her majesty over there didn't teach you the number one rule in combat? Expect the unexpected. Now let's start again."

Persephone shoots a glare at Hades, who covers her laughter with her fist. The wind picks up at Persephone's feet again and she tries to jump out of the way, to kick, to do something, but it still blows her back a few yards. Luckily she doesn't end up on her ass this time.

She lets out a growl.

"There she is!" Minthe says, grinning.

"I'm going to wipe that smug look off your face."

"Oooh, big words from a little princess-" A vine tendril smacks Minthe right across the cheek. Persephone had summoned it from the branches above, curling down like a lackadaisical snake.

"You're in trouble now, Seph," Hades calls, smiling from ear to ear. The bastard is having the time of her life.

Minthe narrows her eyes, bringing her hands up in front of her body. She's summoning the wind, about to do something much bigger before. Persephone panics. She's done plenty of restraining with vines, so she tries that. Minthe seems to expect it. Brings her hands down in a sharp "x" maneuver and the vines are severed.

"Shit." Shit shit shit. All she'd done thus far had to do with plants – stem and petal and root. If Minthe's powers can sever easily through those, what is she to do? She glances at Hades, who keeps her face impassive. She is expecting something, and Persephone's coming up empty-handed.

A huge gust of wind throws her back in the air and her limbs flail. She manages to grow a soft bed of moss to land on before she hits the ground, but it still knocks the breath out of her.

"Come on. You can do more than that," Minthe taunts. Persephone can feel her cheeks heating up at the embarrassment of it all. She gets up and dusts herself off. Thinks. Vines won't work, so other vegetation likely won't either. What is left? She was made from a goddess of the harvest and a god of the sky. She blinks. A god of the sky. Children laugh in the distance hopping from shadow to shadow in the dappled sunlight. Old friends sunbathe in the grass. She brought it to them, without ever meaning to.

Just as Minthe sends another gust at her ankles, Persephone closes her eyes. She feels the familiar tingle of the plant life at her fingertips, and the sun that flows through them. She feels the warmth upon her skin and the freckles on her nose and the lighter gold strands in her hair and she reaches out and touches it. She can see it in her mind, a bright wall inside her. It ripples at her fingertips.

It's hot and soft.

"Now's not the time to meditate," Minthe calls, but Hades hushes her. They sound far away.

Persephone reaches out again, pressing her entire palm to the wall. It gives a bit, and her heart races. She brings her other palm up as well, and *pushes*. Whatever is holding the wall up seems to break, and the light rushes around her like a flood. She gasps and steps back, but there's no getting away from it. Not that she needs to, anyways. It is welcoming her, holding her, this liquid sunlight. Something in her heart cracks open and lets out a startled laugh. It feels good. It feels free.

When she opens her eyes again, Hades and Minthe are staring at her. Minthe speaks to Hades, something like worry limning her face, but Persephone can't hear them. She just hears the sunlight, and it sounds like the strumming of a harp. She brings her palms up like Minthe had minutes before, and pushes what is within her, *out*. A thick beam of sunlight hits Minthe square in the chest and she is knocked all the way to the other side of the garden, meters away. Persephone slowly comes back to herself. She looks at her hands, trembling. Her fingertips are glowing gold, like the sunlight is swimming under skin. Minthe, a tiny figure across the field, stumbles to her feet.

"Is she okay?" Persephone asks, voice hoarse.

Hades waves to Minthe, and she waves back. "She's fine, baby." Hades is beside Persephone, staring at her hands too.

"Did you know that was going to happen?" Persephone whispers.

"No, I didn't. I suspected there was something," she trails off. "But I didn't know for sure."

"But you set me up against her knowing my power would be useless. The other power, I mean."

"I thought you'd find a different way to use it. I didn't know you'd pull out an entirely new ability."

Minthe reaches them, having limped her way over.

"Damn, princess!"

Persephone, still in shock, asks, "Are you alright?"

"Nothing some rest and rum won't fix. Unless you want to kiss it better?"

"Minthe," Hades rumbles.

"Sorry, sorry." She puts her hands up in surrender. "You're no fun, H. She pushed me halfway across the underworld, it's the least she could do."

Even though she knows Minthe is joking, Persephone groans and covers her face with her hands. "I'm sorry!"

"It's okay. It will take a lot more than that to take me out." Minthe pats her on the back.

"You should be proud," Hades says. "You literally unleashed a power you never knew you had. Not many people can say they have more than one connection to the celestial."

Persephone peeks at her through her fingers. "Are you sure?"

"Yes. And between you and me," she moves closer, hand up as if telling Persephone a secret, "she deserved it."

"I can hear you," Minthe says.

"You might deserve it too," Persephone says, dropping her hands to rest on her hips. "Was it funny? Watching me get knocked on my ass?"

Minthe cackles somewhere over Persephone's shoulder, and Hades furrows her brow, the picture of innocence.

"It's a part of training, love. What was I to do?" She asks, ever the actor.

Persephone stares her down until her facade cracks and she has to look away to keep from laughing, except she catches Minthe's eye and it's over. The two of them can't help themselves. They're laughing at her, hard.

"You are both insufferable. I need a drink." Persephone walks away from them, to find something strong in the kitchen to ease her nerves. Using so much power, one that is entirely new to her, has exhausted her.

By dinnertime, she has forgiven them. How could she not? Hades has those big brown eyes and Minthe has that charming smile. They baked her a cake topped with strawberries and brought it out at dinner and plied her with icing and jokes.

She wasn't really all that mad with them to begin with, anyway. Mainly overwhelmed with the knowledge of her power, and the ramifications of it. People ask her about it at dinner. Most of the people who live in and around the castle either saw her use her power on Minthe, or heard about it through the grapevine - which seems to be a very quick grapevine. Zina asks her if she can burn people (she doesn't know, hopefully not), Voleta asks if she has any other powers related to the sky, like making it rain (she doesn't think so), and Ismeni asks her to do a small demonstration, up close. This, Persephone is able to oblige and more than happy to. After a lifetime of having no power, it's reassuring to have so many people around her excited about it. She focuses and summons a small ball of light in one palm, even rolls it from hand to hand. Zina makes as if to poke it, to which Persephone panics and loses her grip on the power, the little light blinking out.

"Don't touch it," she says, and Zina jerks back. "Sorry, I just don't know if it could hurt you."

"That's amazing," Voleta breathes.

"How odd," Ismeni muses, "That a child of the harvest and the thunder should have power over the sun."

"Zeus is god of the sky, not just thunder," Zina points out. "There's no telling what all you can do!"

Persephone isn't sure she wants to do anything else. She injured Minthe, though Minthe brushes it off. If there's another power she doesn't know about, and it unleashes at the wrong time, she could hurt people.

"So what does this make you the god of?" Sofia asks. "Apollo already lords over the sun."

"I'm not sure," Persephone admits. She doesn't even

know if she wants to be a god. Powers seem nice, yes. And she'd like to be able to help people. But as far as having the authority that gods have? It's too much. "Would anyone like a slice of cake?"

Luckily her new friends stop asking her questions. They go back to various conversations about new garments in style in the village, mortal political news, though nothing to do with the small kingdom Persephone comes from, and in general just chatting. She didn't have much family, at least not family that she saw regularly growing up. It makes her observe in bittersweet silence the easy back and forth of these people who all know each other and all love each other.

She's distracted by Hades touching her hand.

"Are you alright?" she asks in a low voice.

Persephone nods, smiling a little. "I'll just miss them, if things in the mortal realm don't go well."

"What do you mean, 'if things don't go well'? I won't let anything happen to you."

"I have to fight on my own, or he'll never understand." she shakes her head, still looking at the folks gathered around the table.

"Understand *what*?" Hades seems genuinely perplexed, and perhaps a bit angry, though Persephone's not sure which part of it she's angry with.

"I think...he already sees me as an object. If you get involved, he will see it as a fight over a thing, between two monarchs who wish to own it."

"I don't wish to own you."

"I know. But he does, and he'll assume you do too. I want to do it so he has no choice but to *see* me." She looks into Hades' eyes, so old and young at the same time. "Do you understand?"

"I do." She nods, entwining their fingers. "You may fight your own battles, but if it comes down to it, I will end his life to save yours without a second thought."

The expression on her face is so intense that

Persephone looks down at her plate, heart pounding. It's disorienting, to have someone love her so fiercely.

"Persephone," Hades murmurs. "Look at me."

She does, after a breath.

"I see you," Hades says.

Her eyes begin to prickle with tears and she has to look away again. There's an unnamable emotion welling in her chest, both heavy and light, both sad and elated. Relieved and afraid. She wants to wrap her arms around her and never let go. But they are at dinner and their friends are chatting and laughing just feet away and she still has one strawberry left to eat.

"I see you too," she says.

Hades smiles that sweet, toothy smile that belongs more to a roguish farmer's daughter than a goddess of the underworld, and Persephone smiles too.

She decides she's done waiting. She wants to go to the mortal realm tomorrow and sort all of this out. Because she's tired of there being a "but" to her happiness, of not being able to open her heart as wide as she wants to. Tomorrow she'll save Lila, sort out her mother, and give Aetius whatever she decides he deserves.

Hades must see the change in her expression because her smile drops and her jaw flexes. There's worry on her face. "You want to go."

"Yes."

"When?"

"Tomorrow."

She expects surprise or a rebuttal, but she shouldn't have. Hades sees her. And so she nods once, squeezes her hand, stands up and proposes a toast to the whole table.

"To our Persephone," she calls. "The woman who brought us the sun!"

"To our sun!" someone calls out, and she could begin weeping right there. They all repeat in unison, in celebration "To our sun!"

She knows her face is probably glowing red. She can

feel it, the shyness, the embarrassment. But it's not bad. Hades wraps her arm around her shoulder and tucks her into her side. She lets herself cry as she takes a swig of her wine. Cry for all of these people who love her, and who she loves.

CHAPTER 26

Later that night, she looks around her room, trying to memorize each nook and cranny and detail. Persephone should be sleeping, to prepare for tomorrow. But she's jittery, anxious. She bites her nails and paces her room and tries to imagine how it will all go. She chose not to send word of her arrival tomorrow, hoping for the element of surprise. That doesn't mean Aetius won't have the kingdom's entire army at his disposal, or that her mother won't come running the second she senses Persephone in the mortal realm. It doesn't guarantee Lila's safety.

She wonders if Lila has heard of everything that's happened. What she thinks of it. Does she resent Persephone for this? Did she miss her at all? Did she ever regret her decision to go along with her father?

Useless questions. Useless worrying. Persephone wants to rake her nails down her face, the way she would do as a young girl when she was frustrated, but that would fix nothing and worry Hades.

Hades. That sweet, ridiculous goddess.

After the music she asked the room, or rather told the room, "How about a party?" And everyone, warm and fuzzy from their drink of choice, had cheered the affirmative. Various stringed instruments and a panpipe or two were produced, and thus began the revelry that lasted upwards of three hours. Persephone danced until her feet hurt and sang until her voice got scratchy, with everyone. She and Hades danced properly, not the formal, slow swaying of the ball. But actual feet-moving, hip-swaying, giggly dancing. She misses Hades now, though it's maybe been forty-five minutes since the party dispersed. She wonders what she's up to. If she's thinking of Persephone the way she's thinking of her. This could be her last night here. She doesn't want to spend it alone.

She glances in the mirror, making sure her hair isn't in too much of disarray. Logically she knows that Hades has seen her at her worst and still wants her, but somehow she still feels the need to look alright. She had bathed after the party and put on a nightdress. It's a soft, comfortable thing that's utterly shapeless. It won't do. She looks through her wardrobe and finds one that's pale pink, with a low neckline. It hugs her body in all the right places, framing her décolletage. It flares out a bit at the waist and ends mid-thigh. She smiles at her reflection. No matter what Hades says, Persephone may never be able to see her again after tomorrow. She could die, or be trapped, or anything really. And she loves Hades and she loves the way she makes her feel, not just her but also her body. She wants to take back what was stolen from her by a lesser man. So she wraps the robe Hades gave her on top of the nightdress, and takes a deep breath.

She peeks her head out the door, and when she sees that the coast is clear she slips out. The smooth stones are cool against her feet and she snuggles deeper into the robe. She can do this. She can do this. She will do this.

She knocks softly on Hades' door, but the sound echoes around the hallway and she winces. She doesn't want to alert the entire castle to her...comings and goings. The large doors swing open. Hades' bedroom seems empty, though.

She steps in and says, "Hello?"

"In here." Her voice comes from the bathroom.

Persephone leans against the bathroom doorway to find Hades in front of the bathroom mirror, scissors raised in her hand. She's just in her trousers and bandeau again, Persephone is pleased to see.

"Are you cutting your hair?"

"Yes."

"You don't have people to do that for you?"

Her shoulders sag a bit. "I don't know what else to do, to be honest. I thought it might be a good distraction."

"Distraction from tomorrow?"

"Yes."

"You're so powerful. What do you have to be scared of?"

Hades puts the scissors down and looks at her. "There are so many ways tomorrow could go. And, if you decide to stay there for some reason, I have to be prepared for that."

"I don't want to stay there."

"You may say that now, but I know how much you love your mother, and how much she loves you. Your mind may change when you see her. Or maybe it will change when you see Lila. It's been a long time, hasn't it?"

"Are you jealous?"

"No. You deserve to have a mother and you deserve to have your old friend. I'm not jealous of them, I-" her mouth opens and closes, at a loss for words. "I just don't know what I'd do without you. But I know that it's your decision, and I will respect whatever you decide to do when this is all over."

"And if I don't survive?"

"Why would you say that?"

"It's a very real possibility."

"You will survive."

"But if I don't?"

"You *will*, Persephone."

"You can't know for sure."

"If you die, I'll burn the world to the ground." She says it so matter-of-factly.

Persephone frowns though her heart beats tenfold. "Is that a threat? That's not a very good plan."

"Dying is not a very good plan either."

"I'm not planning to-"

"What are you planning to do?"

She crosses her arms over her chest. "Sneak into the castle, find Lila, and then incapacitate the bastard?"

"And how will you sneak in?"

She huffs. "Find an inconspicuous opening and *sneak* in."

Hades shakes her head, looking back at her reflection.

"You don't trust me to take care of myself?"

"I trust you, Persephone. I don't trust them."

"Them?"

"That sniveling prick and his masses. Your mother. Any mortal who may sell you out for a reward from him. I've seen the worst of what humanity has to offer, you forget." Her knuckles are white, her gripping the counter so hard.

"But also the best, right?" Hades doesn't respond, just stands there with her eyes closed. Persephone walks over and peels her hands away from the counter. She hops up on the counter in front of her, beside the basin, and turns her face towards her. Hades' eyes open at Persephone's touch on her cheek. Persephone picks up the scissors, a sharp, wicked looking thing, and asks, "Will you show me how?"

Hades huffs and nods. "The best indeed," she mutters. She shows Persephone how to pull strands of hair aside in her fingers, and how to cut the jagged ends in quiet little snips. How to follow the angle of her jawline. In no time Persephone's inches away from Hades' jaw, biting her bottom lip as she concentrates on cutting her hair. Her knees rest against Hades' sides, and she holds her waist. At one point Hades starts tracing circles with her thumb, and it ventures close enough to the juncture of Persephone's leg and hip that she jerks and accidentally nicks her cheek.

She drops the scissors and wipes the blood away. "I'm so sorry!"

"It's okay." Hades doesn't flinch when she pats a wet cloth to the cut, so it can't be too deep. "Are you ticklish?"

She cringes. "Yes, but I hate being tickled. I *hate* it."

Hades hums in response, sliding her hands away.

"No!" Persephone grabs her wrists and brings her hands back to her waist, firm. "That doesn't mean you can stop touching me." That finally gets a smile out of Hades. Good. Persephone doesn't like seeing her worried or stressed or so solemn. "Just don't tickle me, okay? I mean it."

"I won't, baby." And how simple it was, to have Hades listen to her. She finishes her hair, brushing the hairs off of her shoulders and neck. After she's done, Hades instructs her to apply some sort of liquid concoction through her hair, and she can almost see it get shinier with ever stroke. It smells like pine and she realizes it must be the reason Hades smells like that all the time.

"Did you need something, when you came in here earlier?" she asks Persephone.

"I just wanted to see you."

"Well I'm glad you did." She wraps her hands beneath Persephone's knees to slide her closer. She kisses her cheek, then her jaw, then her neck. Three quick things that could lead to more, or not. It's all up to her.

"Can I sleep with you tonight?" Persephone blurts out. "Can I sleep in your bed, I mean? With you?"

"The answer to that question will always be yes."

She exhales a breath she didn't know she'd been holding. "Thank you."

Hades waves off her thanks and picks her up from the counter. Persephone squeaks at the sudden movement, wrapping her legs and arms around her tightly though she knows she'd never let her fall. No matter how many times Hades picks her up, she still feels the split-second panic that she may be too heavy. But her lover is strong. She supposes that must be what she is to her, now. Lover. It feels a bit odd to admit to herself.

Hades drops her on the bed and she laughs as she bounces a bit.

"Are you going to sleep in that?" she asks, gesturing at the robe.

"Um...no?" Persephone sounds uncertain, even to herself.

Hades cocks her head to the side.

"No. I'm not," she says, trying to sound more assured. She sits up and unties the belt, then shrugs the fabric off of her shoulders. She glances up at Hades and she takes it all the way off, goosebumps erupting on her arms in the chill air.

Hades' eyes travel over her chest and the length of her legs, dark and hungry. Part of her wants to cover up but the other part...wants to lay back, lean on her elbows. Let her look her fill. She doesn't usually feel proud of her body, especially when it's so exposed. But Hades is looking at her like she's a treasure trove and a four-course-meal and also just...someone she loves very much.

Hades is silent, and Persephone feels pinned by her gaze. She can't stand it anymore and blurts out, "Is this okay?" By all means, if she doesn't want this, Persephone doesn't want to make her feel pressured, but she gets the feeling that she does want this.

"It's more than okay." Hades' voice is lower than usual, a bit gravelly. She crawls onto the foot of the bed and makes her way up Persephone's body, gently pushing her shoulders down to the mattress until her head is caged by her arms. Persephone's heart pounds even harder, which she didn't think was possible. "Is this okay?" Hades asks, holding herself over Persephone.

Persephone nods, parting her legs so Hades can settle between them.

"Words please," she says.

"Yes, it's okay," Persephone huffs. To prove her point, she wraps a leg around one of Hades' to pull her closer. Hades obliges, pressing against her. The seam of her pants press against Persephone's core, and she shudders. She had forgotten how good it felt, how Hades felt. Not just her hips against her own but the weight of her whole body, comforting and safe.

"Is that an attitude I detect?" Hades kisses at her jaw, and she sighs in bliss. The danger of her words escapes Persephone until she bites her neck - not hard enough to injure but with just enough pressure to shock her. And shock her, it does. A wave of arousal hits her and she bucks her hips against Hades'.

"You like being bitten?"

"I-I guess so?" Persephone breathes.

Hades grins, and Persephone sees a flash of the formidable legend that terrifies mortals. Granted, she's also terrified. But it's delicious. Hades ducks her head back down to suck at Persephone's neck, her collarbone, and the valley between her breasts. She intersperses the kisses with gentle bites that make Persephone's breath catch.

She tangles her fingers in Hades' hair, scratching lightly at her scalp.

Hades looks up at her, panting. "Can I touch you here?" Her face hovers above Persephone's chest.

"Yes," she says, so quickly she's a bit embarrassed.

Hades seems to think for a second, then asks, "Can I kiss you here?"

Persephone swallows, then nods. "Yes. Yes to everything, just stop - stopping! Please."

She narrows her eyes. "You will tell me if you need me to stop, right?"

"Yes. Thank you."

Hades looks at her face for a few more seconds, as if

making sure she's being truthful. Once she decides she believes her, she scatters kisses over the tops of her breasts, exposed by the nightgown. Her hand travels from Persephone's knee, up her thigh and waist, and finally over her breast, squeezing and kneading. The other hand pulls down the top until her breasts are exposed. And though Persephone has been self-conscious of them, their sag and the size of her areolas and the hair that most people have, she had read in a book once, but it hadn't helped her self-esteem - despite all of this, Hades seems to adore them. She sucks her right nipple into her mouth and Persephone's back arches. Her tongue laves around the hardened peak as her hand pinches the other. It feels so strange and warm and wet and the sensation zings through Persephone's body straight to her core. Hades switches sides and her toes curl. After a bit she kisses the valley between her breasts and pulls her gown down, down, until Persephone grabs her hands. A flash of panic crosses her mind as she thinks of the swell of her stomach, the hair there too, the dip between her waist and thighs, the jiggle of her flesh when she moves. She thinks back to Aetius, grabbing one of her rolls and guffawing, "Oh my god, what did you eat? Is this a pastry?"

"What's wrong, baby?" Hades asks.

"I just, I don't know. I'm sorry," she says, flustered. "It's my stomach."

"What about it?"

"Everything," she huffs. She regrets her outburst earlier, telling Hades to stop stopping. What a flake she must look like now. But the worst part is that she wants her - wants her to do everything she wants with her, but it's so *hard* to let go.

"You are worried I'll think you are ugly?"

Her face flushes red, because that's exactly what she's worried about. She covers her face with her hands and mumbles, "I guess."

"That's impossible."

"You don't mean that."

"I don't?" Hades pulls Persephone's hands away from her face and makes her look her in the eyes. She looks almost angry, but Persephone doesn't think it's at her. "Do you think I would lie to you?"

Persephone shrugs and looks away. "I'm sorry."

"Don't be sorry. I'm sorry that you think you'd be capable of repulsing me, when I love every inch of you."

She looks quickly back at Hades. The word 'love'. It makes her want to cry, for a multitude of reasons she doesn't have time to examine. "I think you believe what you're saying, but it doesn't make it true." She wants to curse her voice for wobbling.

"Who told you that you were ugly?" It's the softest demand she's ever heard. Hades strokes her thumb across Persephone's cheek, and it soothes her, just a bit.

Girls in the pond when she was only eight, and the wet of her dress clung to her chubby body. The summer she worked in the tavern and the boss drunkenly slurred one night, "Turn around and let me see that ass. If you even have one". And Aetius, over and over again.

"No one had to."

"But someone made you feel it."

"*He* did. But not just him, it's just kind of the way it is."

"In the mortal realm."

"Yes."

"Not here, Persephone. Never here." When Persephone tries to turn her face away from Hades, she cradles her cheek and turns it back. Persephone has no choice but to let the truth, the gravity of Hades' words sink into her bones. "You are sure you won't let me kill him tomorrow?"

"I'll think about it," she says, and she can feel the corner of her mouth lift into a smile, despite herself.

Hades smiles down at her, dragging her thumb across Persephone's bottom lip. "There's my girl."

Persephone wraps her arms around Hades' neck and

pulls her down in a tight embrace. As if she'll fly away if she doesn't hold on. Hades presses a kiss to her shoulder, and another, and another.

"To be clear, I don't have to have this in order to want you. If you told me you never wanted to be touched again, I'd still want you to stay," She traces her index finger over the line of Persephone's nose, and down to the bow of her lips. "But, if you do want this, you have to know that I've got you. I adore you head to toe. So do you want this?"

"I do."

"Then what can I do to prove it to you?" she whispers in her ear, breath tickling her hair.

Persephone hesitates, desperate for Hades to continue, but so, so afraid. "I don't know. I don't know if there's anything."

"Will you let me try?"

Her heart thunders in her chest, but she looks into her goddess's brown eyes and knows she'd do anything for her. So she nods.

"Yes?"

"Yes."

Hades kisses her forehead, and repeats, "I've got you, Persephone."

She takes a deep breath as Hades peels the dress down over her waist, hips, thighs, and off her body completely. All that's left is the underwear.

"As I suspected," she murmurs, skating her hands over Persephone's body, "perfect."

Tears spring into her eyes and Hades bends over her body, kisses her belly, caresses her curves and thighs. It's like she needs to touch every inch of her and she's burning for it. Her lips travel from the swell of her belly to the tops of her thighs, then to the inside of her knee, and up, up, up the insides of her thighs. She leaves wet marks where her lips have been, and when they're exposed to the cool air it makes Persephone shiver.

With every movement Hades makes, the tension within

her coils up more and more, until her core nearly throbs. Though the desire within her feels like a snake about to strike, her body becomes more and more pliant under the ministrations.

"I love your stomach," Hades says. And she sucks a bruise onto her skin, a few inches beside her navel.

"I love your thighs." A hickey to her inner thigh, high up.

She crawls back up so they're face to face. "I could just eat you up." She buries her face in Persephone's neck again and softly bites her shoulder. Persephone runs her fingers along Hades' shoulder blades, down her back and up again.

"Then do it," she whispers. She didn't entirely mean to say it out loud, but she doesn't regret it. Hades looks at her, the challenge in her eyes, and a crooked grin spreads across her face. She looks wicked. It sends even more excitement to her core.

Without another word, she's kissing her hips. Hades pulls down her underwear just a bit, and presses a kiss there too. She looks up at Persephone again, and she nods. So Hades peels down the garment slowly, revealing the dark thatch of curls there and Persephone has to bite her lip to keep from gasping as the cool air hits her cunt. Hades throws her underwear somewhere off to the side and then *dives in*. She licks a wide stripe from Persephone's opening to her clit, and then down again. It feels so foreign and odd and yet so intriguing. Her mouth is hot and wet, and she sucks her labia in a very particular way that has her legs beginning to tremble. She plunges her tongue inside Persephone and her hips buck. Hades presses a forearm over her hips to keep her from moving too much, the other hand squeezing her ass. She feels like she's about to jump out of her skin, and she has to close her eyes. She covers her mouth with her hand to keep from making noise. Hades stops suddenly and Persephone's eyes fly open, worried that something's wrong. That she'll tell her she's changed her mind because she doesn't taste good or doesn't smell good-

"I want to hear you when I make you cum," she says. "So take your hand off your mouth and stop holding back."

Persephone didn't know she could be even more embarrassed, considering she's shown Hades everything, but her cheeks feel hot nonetheless. It's something about the way her lips wrap around the vulgar word.

"Can you do that for me?"

Persephone nods and brings her hand down.

"My good girl."

"Can I - can you hold my hand?"

"Of course, my love."

Hades intertwines her fingers with Persephone's, and Persephone slips her other hand into Hades' dark locks. Then the goddess gets back to work. Although, Persephone had heard that if you love the work you do, you never work a day in your life. And Hades seems to be thoroughly enjoying the work she's doing.

She sets a rhythm across Persephone's clit with her tongue, sucking on it at the same time.

"Oh, fuck," Persephone hisses, and her legs clamp around Hades' head for a second before she realizes and pulls them away.

"You taste divine," Hades murmurs against her. A wave of relief washes over her, but she cannot respond at the moment.

Hades takes away the arm that held Persephone down and she feels her fingertips at her entrance. She teases her with her middle finger, pushing just inside and no further. She gently pumps like that for a bit, making her walls clench and her heart stutter.

Persephone growls and tries to grind down on her finger

Hades lifts her head to croon, "Is my princess feeling bossy?"

"Your princess is tired of your teasing," she huffs.

"Aw. Poor baby. I'll have to fix that." She slides her finger all the way in. Persephone had expected some pain, a pinch, some sort of discomfort. But no. She's got her wet enough that it slides in without much resistance. She plays her body like an instrument she's known her whole life. Her fingers are a bit longer than Persephone's, and it feels so good inside. But she wants more. She wants to be filled up. She shakes as Hades pumps in and out, putting her head back down to suck at her clit.

"Oh, gods," Persephone pants.

"Think you can take another?"

"I-I think." The truth is, she can barely think at all. But she wants more of Hades in every way she can get it.

Persephone squeezes Hades' other hand as she adds a second finger. This time it does sting a bit as it slides in, and she draws in a breath. Hades stops immediately.

"Am I hurting you my love?"

"It's okay. You're just big. Please keep going."

Hades scatters kisses across Persephone's inner thigh as she pushes back in slowly, and when Persephone winces again she dives back down and sucks - hard. Persephone gasps and barely notices when she pushes all the way inside. Then oh- it's ridiculous how good it feels. She pumps her fingers and keeps attacking Persephone's clit with her tongue and lips, and every once in a while the barest brush of teeth, that all too soon she feels the telltale tightening in her stomach that means she's getting close to the edge.

"Hades," she moans.

"Are you going cum for me?"

She nods frantically. "Yes."

"Good. Cum on my fingers like a good girl," she growls, and her tongue is back on her clit.

A few more pumps of her fingers, filling Persephone up so nicely, and the hot wet pressure of her tongue on her clit make her legs once again clamp around her head, and she lets out a moan as sparks fill her body. In those moments all she can think about is the heavenly sensation of Hades sliding wetly inside her and her tongue against her. It might be the most intense orgasm she's ever had. She pulses around Hades' fingers and then the pleasure plateaus gently into a sated, sleepy feeling. She's left panting, feeling boneless.

Hades crawls up her body to look at her. She wipes her face with the back of her hand. "Do you think you can handle one more round, angel?"

"I don't think I can move," Persephone whispers, voice hoarse. Men in the village would laugh loudly about the women they'd been with, what they did and neglected to do in bed. Aetius had expected her to enact some pleasures upon him, even if he had to hurt her to do it. "It's not fair to you."

"You don't have to move. You can just lay there, looking pretty as a portrait," Hades caresses her cheek with her palm, and she nuzzles into it. "Or are you tired, my love?"

And her goddess, her sweet, beautiful giant of a woman, would leave herself aching and unfinished if Persephone was too tired. It's so simple to Hades, to accept her as she is and what she wants, to not pressure Persephone for her own pleasure. She's so unused to it. And she still wants Hades inside her. Even after Hades gave her the biggest orgasm of her life. In fact, now that she's had her, she's not sure she'll ever get enough.

"I want you to fuck me," Persephone says into the darkness of Hades' bedroom, which is starting to feel like theirs. She closes her mouth around Hades' thumb and sucks. And the way she looks at Persephone in that moment, Persephone doesn't think anyone's ever looked at her like that and is sure no one else ever will again. Her eyes are dark, worshipful and hungry.

"Say it again."

"I want you. To fuck me."

"Good girl." Hades nips at Persephone's jaw and rises from the bed.

"Where are you going?" Persephone tries, and fails to keep the whine out of her voice.

"I'll be back. Stay right there."

Persephone huffs and tries to calm her racing mind while she is gone. Hades spends about a minute in the closet and then comes back out, climbing back over Persephone immediately.

She leans down over Persephone on her elbows, and kisses her. She opens her legs for Hades to settle between them, and feels something…different. Something hard against her. It feels wonderful.

"What is that?" she asks, wiggling her hips up against it.

"A strap-on."

"Come again?"

"You will."

Persephone rolls her eyes. "You know what I meant."

"It's an artificial appendage that I can fuck you with." Persephone's eyes go wide, and Hades adds, "If you like."

Hades' fingers had felt good enough inside her, and she's curious what sensation this will bring. Hades has never hurt her. She trusts her. So she says, "I would."

Then Hades' tongue is in Persephone's mouth and against her tongue and she grinds up against her, just the slightest bit. Hades bites her bottom lip gently. Persephone reaches down to unbutton her trousers, fumbling with shaking hands, and curses.

"I've got it," Hades says, through a smile. Persephone helps her shove them down her waist and off completely. Her eyes widen when she sees how big the appendage is. It's made of glass, tinted pink, thick and long. It's attached to a harness that Hades has belted around her waist and thighs. Persephone is genuinely unsure if it will fit. Hades grabs a bottle from the drawer in her bedside table, and pours a generous heaping of a honey-like substance onto the appendage.

"This will help it go in."

"How will this pleasure you?" Persephone asks.

"There is something on the end that's attached to me, that will brush up against me as I fuck you."

"Oh."

"Are you nervous?"

"Yes. And excited."

"No need to fret, little flower. I told you I've got you."

Persephone's worries melt away as Hades' lips meet her neck and she sucks gentle marks onto her skin. The thought flashes through her mind that she'll be black and blue come morning. What a sight for her enemies. Oh well. She can't be bothered to give a fuck when Hades is touching her like this, when her body is on hers and she feels tethered to the earth for once in her life. When she is loved, and loves in return.

Hades lines herself up with Persephone's entrance. And pushes in.

It feels even bigger than it looks, but there's little pain. Persephone hides her face in Hades' shoulder, which she knows she doesn't want her to hide, but she can't help it. She breathes through the stretch. Hades' fist clenches the sheets beside her head, and she grunts on her last push. Then she's fully seated. Persephone exhales. She thought she felt full with two of her fingers inside of her, but this... this is fullness.

"Are you okay, baby?"

She nods and Hades pulls her face so she's looking into her eyes. "Words, please."

"I'm okay. You can move."

Hades rests her forehead against hers and closes her eyes as she pulls out slightly and thrusts again. Persephone watches Hades above her. Her dark hair hanging around her face and her plush lips and here strong jaw. She brings her hands up and into her hair, making her nostrils flare. Her thrusts are slow, but steady.

"You can go faster," Persephone whispers. "I won't break."

Hades' head drops to her shoulder, then. She picks up the pace. The friction of her is so delicious that Persephone feels her eyes roll back, which is embarrassing, so she closes them.

"You're taking it so good, angel," Hades groans. "So good for me." Her hand grabs Persephone's thigh and hitches it around her waist. It makes the angle even deeper, and they both groan. She bites Persephone's shoulder like she did earlier, just a little harder, and Persephone grips her hair tighter.

Hades is still too composed for her liking. She wants her shaking, speechless like she had her. She wraps both legs around her and hisses in her ear, "You can make love to me later. Now fuck me."

"You don't know what you're asking, little flower," Hades growls in her ear. "I don't know if you can handle it."

Persephone huffs when Hades gives her a particularly hard thrust. "I think you're afraid you can't handle it." She doesn't know what has come over her, only that she wants to see her unhinged.

"You want me to fuck you? Fine. I'll fuck you." Hades says. "But when you it gets to be too much, say pomegranate."

"It won't be too much-"

"Do you understand me?"

"I-"

"Do. You. Understand. Me."

"Yes."

"I'm going to hold your wrists down," Hades says, and grabs Persephone's hands from her hair to press them into the bed. She doesn't move again for a few seconds, inspecting Persephone's reaction. She wiggles her wrists experimentally and they don't budge. She waits for panic, or fear, or anxiety, but none of that comes. There's a fluttering in her belly, but she likes it. She gives Hades a small smile, and she takes it as her cue.

She starts pounding.

Persephone lets out sharp breaths with each thrust she takes, so overwhelmed with the friction and fullness that she isn't able to do much else. The breaths devolve into little whines and moans that she never thought she'd let fall from her lips. But it's so much and so right-

"Not so bratty now, are you?" Hades grunts. She arranges Persephone's wrists together above her head and holds them with one hand, and lifts her hips with the other. It hits something deep within her that she didn't know existed.

"Oh, fuck," she groans.

"Good girl. Let me hear you."

She has little choice in the matter. She couldn't keep quiet during this if she tried. Each thrust shoves her up the bed a bit, that's how hard Hades is fucking her.

"My beautiful girl. You're going to make me cum." The growl in Hades' voice is delicious.

Persephone feels it too, a second orgasm building up. Whatever spot Hades is hitting within her, coupled with the way her pelvis grinds against her clit, is driving her wild.

"So you like that, princess?"

She's so blissed out that it takes her to register the question, and Hades growls, "Come on, stay with me baby."

"Yes," she pants out. "Yes, yes yes."

"Fuck," Hades hisses. The pressure builds up in Persephone's pelvis almost to the breaking point. Hades must be close, too, because she lets go of her wrists to bring both hands to her hips, pulling her down onto the strap at the same time that she thrusts. Persephone's glad for it, because now she can hold on to her for dear life.

"Are you going to cum again?" Hades demands, more than asks. She must feel the shaking of Persephone's legs around her.

"Mm-hmm," she moans.

"Then cum for me, princess," she growls in her ear. And everything within Persephone seizes up. Her toes curl and her legs tense and it feels like sparks are shooting out from where they are joined. Hades fucks her through it, kissing her neck. A few thrusts later and she grunts loudly, shuddering. Her hair tickles the side of Persephone's face as she comes and Persephone relishes the feeling. The thought comes to her in a daze, how wicked she has become. How greedy. She wants everything Hades has to give.

They come down together, Hades resting her forehead on Persephone's shoulder. It's so quiet now. She pulls out of her and she misses it instantly. She rests her whole body on Persephone's, propping her head up with one hand, and they lie there, catching their breath. Persephone loves the weight of her.

"Are you okay, sweetheart?" Hades asks. Whatever devil took over her has retreated, for now, leaving the gentleness once more.

Persephone takes stock of herself. Tired, wet, sweaty. But sated. A little shell-shocked perhaps. "I'm good," she says. She thinks about it, trying to detect any lie in her own words, conscious or not. But she finds that she means it. And it may be the first time she's ever felt good after sex with another person. "How are you?"

Hades smiles down at her. "Good." She kisses her on the forehead and makes to get off the bed. Persephone grabs her hand, squeezing hard. She must read the alarm in her face because she says, "I'll be right back. I'm getting a cloth."

Persephone only loosens her grip a fraction of an inch. She knows she is being ridiculous but at the moment losing any contact with her feels horrible.

"Okay," Hades says, nodding. Persephone thought maybe she'd crawl back in bed with her but instead she scoops her up to take with her, making sure she wraps her legs around her waist. Persephone holds on to Hades tight, resting her chin on her shoulder. She's so grateful that Hades doesn't comment on her clinginess. They clean themselves and perform the nightly ablutions, and then crawl back into bed. She has never slept in a bed with a lover before - a naked woman at that. Aetius would do what he wanted and then leave, or make her leave. It was humiliating and left her feeling like a shell of a person. But as she lies in Hades' bed, and she pulls her in close, nuzzling into her hair, she feels completely present.

She's nearly asleep when Hades speaks.

"Persephone, if you choose to stay in the mortal world tomorrow, it cannot be because of his threats. Or your mother guilting you. You have to choose it because you want to be there."

She doesn't respond.

"I know you're awake," Hades says.

"That's easier said than done."

"No. Persephone? Listen to me. I know you want to do this on your own but if it comes down to it, I will not let them force you. And I won't be able to apologize for stepping in."

"There's no point in arguing with you, is there?"

"Absolutely not."

Persephone nods. Snuggles deeper into her chest.

"Do you really think I'd choose to stay up there of my own volition?"

"I don't know. There must be something or someone you miss."

My mother, but the version of the mother I miss is not the one I have. Lila sometimes, but she's long gone anyway.

"My cat Zymi. But other than that, no." She changes the subject. "Thank you for listening to me, tonight. And always. I'm not used to it, but you know that somehow."

"What do you mean listen to you?"

"Just being kind with me. With my body. Not forcing

anything."

"I wish you'd stop thanking me for things that are baseline necessities. I would never, ever, force you. No one should have ever forced you."

"You knew, before my own mother. And I didn't even tell you. How?"

"Something similar happened to me."

Her breath catches.

"My, um. Kronos. Father. I was very young."

"I'm so sorry."

"I think it's why I was given the underworld. I was always a bit unhappier than Poseidon or Zeus, a bit estranged from the things around me. Kept to myself, the dark."

"Do they know?"

"Yes, but it's not talked about. It's shameful to them. Not just that it happened but that I live to bear the evidence. Mortals and demi-gods would doubt us if they knew I was weak enough to let that happen, in their eyes."

"But you were just a child. What could you have done, even as a god? You didn't know."

She gives a sardonic smile and shrugs. "That's not why I'm telling you this."

Persephone frowns at her, dazed and heartbroken and so, so angry for her.

"The way the men in the village spoke of you, and the way you spoke of him, I just knew."

Persephone's bottom lip begins to tremble and she can't stop it. She can't stop the tears that form in her eyes and the thickness of her voice when she asks, "How do you live with it?"

Hades looks at her, so serious and so gentle. "I've had centuries to heal. You have not." She strokes her hair. "You feel guilty about it, don't you? Like it's somehow your fault."

"Yes."

"It wasn't. It isn't. It will never be your fault. Do you

understand me?"

Persephone nods against Hades' chest, tears soaking into her skin. But she doesn't understand. Not quite yet. She wants to bathe in her words, to hear her say it over and over and over again. She wishes they didn't slip away so soon. She knows she should believe her, but those words can't possibly apply to her. Of all the survivors like her, she must be the exception.

"We should go to sleep," Persephone says.

Hades is so warm as they curl up together, her breath in Persephone's hair and the weight of her arm slung over her waist. She wishes she could climb into her body and live there.

CHAPTER 27

She sleeps lightly. Worry twists knots in her stomach. She tries not to toss and turn too much, tries not to disturb Hades. Sometime in the early, early hours of the morning, she slips out of her embrace and back into her own room. There is a wrinkle in Hades' brow as she sleeps, and Persephone resists the urge to smooth it out. After what she said about not stopping herself from interfering, Persephone doesn't want to wake her. She will find a way up to the mortal realm herself. Hades can't get hurt, and her protection of Persephone can't hurt Lila.

She puts on some of the comfortable trousers Hades had given her, and a blouse. Easy to fight in. Easy to run in. She realizes belatedly that she doesn't have any armor, and briefly considers raiding Hades' closet for some, but it would be all too large for her, and probably too clunky.

She puts her hair up, straps a sword to her hip, and she goes. She wouldn't know how to pilot the chariot, and she can't shadow-hop. So she half walks, half jogs the forested trails to Cerberus. The morning is crisp. The sun, her sun, has not yet poked its head over the horizon.

His tail thumps on the ground when he sees her and then he's bounding over to her, and she narrowly dodges a lick to her face.

"Hi, buddy," she croons, and scratches each of his heads. "You're going to let me through, aren't you? My good boy."

He cocks his heads at her and she's briefly reminded of Hades. Like mother like son(s), she supposes. She hopes Hades will not be too angry at her for sneaking off like this. She really shouldn't have told her she was going at all, should've expected the fierce promise of protection, no matter the cost.

She walks off to the side of the gate, crooning, "Come here, boy." She pats her thighs but he just pants with those big dumb smiles on his faces.

"Fine." She rummages through the small satchel she brought and pulls out a slab of meat she'd swiped from the kitchens. All six ears perk up when Cerberus sees what's in her hand.

"Go get it!" She says, and throws it in the opposite direction of the gates. As expected, he goes bounding after it. She heads for the gates, prepared for them to be locked or otherwise not open to her, but it's like they know her. They open at the slightest touch.

She walks through the cool blackness for a bit, and then there's very dim light up ahead. This in-between place is devoid of sound, devoid of anything. She walks until she can slip through the crevice of not-light, and she sees she's stepped out of a hollow tree, right near the place Hades first found her. It's brighter than it was in the in-between place, but it's still night in the mortal realm. The stars wink at her and the trees rustle as if to welcome her home. She gets the feeling the gates would spit her out wherever she needed to go. Perhaps if she survives the day, she'll go to the ocean.

She is a fool for coming alone, she knows this. But she does what fools do, and continues anyway.

CHAPTER 28

The village is not yet awake, not even the cattle lowe nor the chickens cluck. She walks on the edge of the woods so she can see the village through the trees, and can see if anyone is walking about. Her heart aches, passing the familiar huts and houses and roads.

After a half-hour of walking, she has made it to the copse of trees right outside the castle gates. The gates are closed and guarded by two sleepy-looking soldiers. There are likely more walking the parapets. Going through the front gates would draw too much attention, even if the front gate's guards were incapacitated. She will have to get to the top of the wall, then. She watches and waits, counting roughly five minutes between one guard crossing the side of the wall and the next. Aetius keeps a tight watch. So she creeps around to the side of the castle. Luckily, ivy climbs the pockmarked stone, and she gets to work weaving together a ladder strong enough to withstand her weight. It takes longer than she thought it would, and every once in a while she has to stop what she's doing and flatten herself against the wall as a guard passes overhead. It's either a testament to their stupidity or her good fortune that they don't look directly down, but out in the distance. Aetius must be expecting a big spectacle, some sort of warning before she arrives. He nearly gets one. Her arms and legs tremble the higher she goes on the ladder, but she doesn't allow herself to look down until she's reached the top and swung her legs over. She must have lost track of time on the way up, because she hears a man yell, "Hey!" and looks to see one of the guards running towards her.

She throws her hands up as if in surrender, but it is no surrender at all. Vines shoot across the space to wrap around his mouth and hands and legs, effectively gagging and binding him. He stares at her, wide eyes and screaming, though it's muffled. Her heart pounds in her chest as she looks to see if anyone heard his scream. Unfortunately, the three other guards on the wall have seen her and they come at her from all sides. She curses and closes her eyes, thrusting her hands out. She peeks an eye open to see the vines have listened to her without her really knowing what to tell them to do. The guards are all wiggling on the floor of the walkway, bound and blindfolded and gagged by thick vines. Not enough to hurt them, but enough that they won't be able to get free and raise any alarm. They won't be found until the next soldiers arrive for their shift, and she has no idea when that will be. She resists the urge to whisper "sorry!" to all of them before leaving. A door in one of the parapets leads to a staircase going down. She takes a deep breath, and steps in. She walks as lightly as she can, her boots thudding softly with each step. When she gets to the bottom, she listens for any footsteps, but hears nothing.

She peeks around the corner to see that she is in the courtyard, sprawling and gaudy. The castle itself is right up ahead. It's smaller than Hades' castle, but somehow it looks lifeless. Hades castle was full of bustling life and warm fireplaces and laughing voices, even at night, the castle felt alive. This one does not. It's a dead thing, dressed up to look fancy and rich.

She is not overly familiar with the castle, but she knows Aetius would probably keep Lila in the dungeons. And dungeons were usually at the very bottom of the castle, right? There aren't any guards in the inner courtyard, but she runs across it as fast as she can in case anyone is watching from the windows. She supposed she'll walk around the perimeter of the castle, looking for any openings other than the front door. A few times she thinks she sees shadows through the high windows, and she has to press herself against the castle wall. The guards circle the wall overhead, but they mostly look to the exterior.

Lo and behold she eventually finds a window within reach, just above her eye level. It's dark inside but she knows that bedrooms are usually in the upper levels, so she has her vines lift her up so she can kick it in. It's odd to rest her entire weight on stems, and she loses her balance when she kicks. She tumbles loudly through the window with a few scratches on her, but no one comes running into the room. It looks to be a small library. She puts her ear to the door to listen for anyone coming and going. Perhaps a guard or a servant walks by, but she counts to 60 after they pass and she opens the door. She's in a corridor, long and cold, with a myriad of doors on either side.

So she starts the painstaking process of opening each one a bit, peeking in to see if it leads to any downward stairs. She presses her ears to the wood first, of course, to see if she can hear anyone on the other side. They're mostly empty parlors and closets and the like. She evidently doesn't listen close enough, however. When she opens the last door on the left, she comes face to face with a young girl. Her eyes go wide when she takes in Persephone's attire and sword strapped to her hip and she opens her mouth, but Persephone covers it with her hand before she can scream. She slips into the room the girl was coming out of, which turns out to be a servant's tunnel. Persephone backs the girl up to the wall so she can't run, and she speaks slowly and quietly, "I'm not going to hurt you. Don't scream. I just need you to show me the dungeons. Nod if you understand me."

The girl nods.

"I'm going to take my hand away now. Please don't scream." She takes her hand away. The girl looks at her, chest heaving.

"Who are you?" she whispers.

"It doesn't matter. I just need to get to the dungeons, then I'll be out of your hair."

"Why?"

"That also doesn't matter."

"Why should I help you?"

"Someone I love is imprisoned here, and she has done nothing wrong."

The girl's eyes widen. "You're the woman the prince has been looking for!"

"Shh!"

"Are you here to kill him?"

"I'm here to save my friend."

"You have a sword, though. You could kill him."

"If I promise not to kill the prince, will you take me where I need to go?"

The girl is quiet for a moment. "No."

"What?"

"You must do it. He- he is a horrible man. He's done horrible things. To me, to others-"

"He hurt you?"

The girl nods, gravely. "And I believe he's hurt you too?"

Persephone wants to cry or scream or hug this girl but she's frozen. Her voice cracks when she speaks, "What is your name?"

"Maisie."

"I will kill him, Maisie. I promise you."

The girl nods, tears in her eyes, and turns slowly, beckoning for Persephone to follow. They creep on light feet the whole way, and Persephone quietly thanks the fates that she ran into Maisie. She would have never been able to find it on her own, with the dozens of hallways and staircases and doorways they had to go through. With each level down they go, the air gets mustier and mustier. Then Maisie stops at a particularly dark, grimy door.

"The dungeons are through here. There is a guard down there, but he usually naps during his shift. Can you get past him?"

Persephone nods. "Thank you, so much. I know how risky this is for you."

Maisie takes her hands. They're a bit sweaty, betraying just how anxious the girl is. "Just make sure the risk pays off. Many people are rooting for you."

She slips away quickly and quietly, head down, and Persephone watches her go.

Her heart pounds and the sharp pangs of unease shoot through her stomach as she opens the door and descends the steps. They're slimy, gray limestone. Things scuttle in the darkness, wary of being stepped on.

She's about to see Lila again. It's been so long. Will she hate her, for tangling her in this mess? Is she injured?

Persephone reaches the bottom step, and as Maisie said, the guard is sleeping. He sits on a bench, head leaned back, snores echoing off the dungeon walls. She can see a long stretch of cells perpendicular to the corridor she is currently in. She creeps around him, eyeing the ring of keys on his belt. She needs to make sure Lila is here before making any brash moves. She walks the line of cells. It is a very, very long line. About a third of them have occupants, and they're of all ages and genders. But by their clothes, she can tell they are all poor. Most are sleeping, but a few stare at her as she walks past. They don't speak, neither to alert the guard nor to beg her to set them free. Perhaps too exhausted or defeated. The very last cell, containing a wooden bench for a bed and very little else, contains a sleeping woman. She is turned away from the bars, from

Persephone, but Persephone could recognize the curve of her shoulders and short, chestnut hair anywhere. She'd slept in the same bed as her for years, after all.

CHAPTER 29

Lila is barefoot and dirty. She must have been here for a week at least. Did they feed her? Allow her any baths? Did they torture her?

Persephone can't worry about that right now. She has to get her out. She sneaks back to where the guard is sleeping. She kneels at his side and reaches for the key ring on his belt. He jerks in his sleep, nearly giving her a heart attack, and then she tries again. It's not a complicated mechanism to open the ring, but the keys jingle as she slides it off the belt. She slides them out and they are safely in her hand when a loud commotion comes from the other side of the door, causing her to jump and drop the keys. They clatter to the floor and the guard jerks awake. She grabs the keys while he's still waking up and then before he can open his mouth to scream, he's bound and gagged. He still tries to scream through the thick vine, red faced and wiggly. She's getting better and better at wrapping people like this, but she's not perfect yet. She can hear guards calling to one another in the corridor above. The soldiers from outside must have managed to get free and alert others. She runs to Lila's cell and fumbles with the keys, trying to find the right one.

"Wake up," she hisses. "Lila!"

Lila wakes and peeks over her shoulder, lackadaisical. Weak. "Persephone?"

"Yes. I need you to get up. I'm getting you out."

"Is it really you?" Her voice is scratchy. She gets off the bench and totters over to the bars. Persephone finds the right key finally, and the lock pops open. She throws the cell door wide and - pauses. Two years ago, maybe she would have thrown her arms around Lila. But she is unsure now. They stand face to face.

"It's me. I'm sorry for all of this."

"How did you even get here?"

"It's a long story. You need to go."

"How? It sounds like there are people out there."

"I'll cover you," Persephone says, and tries to inject confidence in her voice. "Just trust me, please."

Lila nods, and starts limping in the direction of the door. Persephone walks behind her, but something stops her. She goes to the next conscious prisoner, an older man with a scraggly beard.

"If I leave these with you, do you promise to free everyone else?" She holds up the keys. "I have to leave."

He nods, roused from his seated position, eyes brighter than before.

"Hurry. I don't know how long the guard will stay bound," she says, and hands them to him through the bars. "I'm sorry I can't do more."

He watches her go with bright, watery eyes but says nothing. She will just have to trust that he will do the right thing.

Then she and Lila stand at the dungeon door. "Stay behind me, okay?" Persephone says.

"What are you going to do?" Lila's brow furrows as it used to when they were kids, and Persephone had come up with a ridiculous plan to steal sweets from the bakery.

"You'll see." Persephone opens the dungeon door, and at first, it seems the coast is clear. She is able to retrace some of the steps Maisie took to lead her down. When they get back up to the ground level, soldiers are pacing. There are at least five of them. Others must be dispersed through the castle, searching for her. She steps out from the corner quietly.

"If you act like you never saw me, I won't have to hurt you," she announces to the room.

They turn to her in unison, raising their weapons. Mostly swords, but one has a crossbow. They all converge on her at once. She throws her hands up and forces thorny stems to grow, wrapping around the hilts of their weapons. They shout and drop them, but not before the one with the bow shoots. Persephone watches it as if time has slowed, headed right for Lila. She lunges to block it, earning her an arrow right in the shoulder. She screams as pain blooms throughout the muscle. But then comes the anger. Her hands are balled into fists and they tremble.

Lila is saying something to her, gasping. Probably worried about the arrow in her shoulder. But Persephone stares at the man who shot it, whose eyes go wide as she gnashes her teeth. The other men back away as a line of poppies erupts from his throat, as if it had been slit with a blade. But instead of the red of blood, there is the red of petals. The man chokes and scratches at his throat, trying to pull out what has taken root inside him.

"Persephone!" Lila yells, and shakes her, jarring the wounded shoulder. The distraction grounds her a bit and the poppies vanish. The man lies on the floor, panting. Blood seeps out from the holes where the stems had once been, but he could heal. Possibly. Hopefully.

The other men look at her with horror and fear, and she suddenly feels like a monster. She pulls Lila down a hallway she vaguely remembers, hoping it's the right direction. They round a corner and run right into another group of soldiers. There's probably fifteen this time.

Persephone doesn't even hesitate. She summons thorns on the hilts of their weapons and the soles of their shoes so when they try to lunge at her, they're in too much pain to succeed. They groan and yell and try to grab at her as she pushes past with Lila in tow, but none of them can lay a finger on her. Because she has grown sleeves of thorns, twining down her arms and chest and legs and the crown of her head. The side of the vine that touches her is smooth. She would do it for Lila, but she is scared Lila will think it an attack or worse, that she would accidentally hurt her somehow. They leave the gaggle of men behind, many of them stumbling after, and the fatigue of using so much of her power starts to catch up with her.

So for the rest of the way out, she peers around corners and watches for shadows below doorways, and waits until they have left before continuing on. Lila is quiet.

They make it to the great hall, but Persephone stops short. It's packed full of soldiers. A general seems to be instructing them. They back up and hide in the first room that has an unlocked door - which seems to be the kitchens. They're nearly as large as the ones at home - or rather, Hades' castle. But it's too clean and austere to be any sort of cozy. Two women pause their hushed conversation, huddled around a small table.

Persephone puts her finger to her lip.

The women stare at her as she looks around. Near the back there is another, smaller door.

"Is there a door to the gardens?" She whispers.

The larger woman nods. "Through the pantry back there. You have an arrow in you, miss."

"Thank you. We were never here, okay?"

"Okay."

As she and Lila creep to the door the woman indicated, Persephone muses that no one except for the soldiers seems to give a rat's ass about Aetius. And if the women do tell someone what they've seen, hopefully Lila will be far from here by then. As they rush through the pantry, Lila grabs random pieces of food and shoves them in the pockets of her dress. Always so smart, Persephone thinks.

Always making up the gaps in judgment that Persephone lacks.

Persephone cracks the side door, and the garden is crawling with soldiers. She gets the sinking feeling that either she or Lila will not make it out, and hopes with all her heart that it's not Lila. She feels the strain on her power so acutely. She's bone-weary, but still able to use it if she needs to. She concentrates and reaches out to the willow trees dotting the garden in the early morning light. The dangling branches spring into action, grabbing the soldiers nearest them, twining around their bodies until they are hanging in the air, kicking and wailing. The rest shout and try to run, and Persephone throws the door wide. She summons rose bushes around them in a wide circle, and then more and more and more until it's a wall about seven feet high of thick, sharp bush. That leaves a few straggling soldiers, three of which run away like deer into the garden. The last one has the audacity to come at her with his sword. She pushes Lila back and whips out her own weapon, conserving what power is left.

Metal clashes with metal, and the soldier, barely a man, hisses a very foul word at her.

The fact of it is that he has been training with swords for far longer than she, and he is a lot less tired than she. He gets one good nick in her side and she growls, calling forth the roots below to wrap around his ankles tight. He yelps, trying to move his legs.

"Release me and fight me, coward!" he screams at her.

"Do yourself a favor and get out of the military," she says. As she sprints away with Lila, he spits curses at her. She wraps roots around his mouth.

She tries a few times to build a ladder up the wall with vines as she did before, but they wilt away. It turns her stomach. Something isn't right. She's tired, but she didn't think she was so tired as to render her power useless. But maybe she reached the bottom of her magic. She tries not to panic, and Lila doesn't comment on it. Lila does insist on breaking off the end of the arrow stuck in Persephone's shoulder, so that there's only a short stub sticking out. The jerking pain of her breaking it makes Persephone bite the inside of her cheek so hard there's blood. After that, they really have no choice but to creep along the castle wall, praying there will be an opening.

"You have powers," Lila pants.

"Yes. You have a tattoo behind your ear."

"Yes. You noticed."

"How did your father allow that?"

"He doesn't know."

"Oh." *I didn't think you were one for rebelling*, is what she wanted to say, but she abstains. There's no time for arguments, for resentments.

"Thank you for saving me," Lila says.

"Don't thank me. I got you into this mess."

"What happened to you, Persephone?"

"What do you mean?"

"I mean, what made you stab a prince?"

"Did he tell you anything?"

"No. The other prisoners whispered about you. I wouldn't be surprised if neighboring kingdoms have heard by now. Apparently everyone knows, but they don't know why."

"The prince gave no official statement?"

"Just that you were treasonous."

"Do they all hate me?"

"No. They spoke of you like a hero."

Persephone shouldn't care what people think of her, and she knows that. But she can't help but feel a bit of relief that it was not only Maisie who thought she did the right thing, even if it's only a few people. She focuses on the ridges of her sword hilt beneath her tight grip so she doesn't tear up. Some hero, crying at the drop of a hat.

"And what do you think?"

"I always worried your…spontaneity would get you into serious trouble one day." she must have noticed

Persephone tensing up. "I don't know what prompted you to do it, and I won't ask, but I know he probably deserved it."

They walk in silence, Persephone's mind running a million miles per hour. Everything that has happened, being in such a dangerous position, having to look out not only for herself, but for Lila as well. It's all put her on high alert. She can't think of anything to say to Lila at the moment, though she's dreamed of meeting her again and dreamed of saying the perfect, right thing to her. It eventually dawns on her that they haven't seen anyone in quite some time. Not even anyone on the ramparts. And they're getting closer to the front courtyard. They're going to have to go through the front entrance.

"I'm getting the feeling this is a trap," she says to Lila.

"I don't think there's any other way we can go."

Persephone focuses on taking deep breaths in and out, in and out. No way out but through. Her shoulder aches, blood drenching the front of her shirt, but she won't take the arrow out for fear of bleeding out. It's okay, she repeats to herself. It will be okay. I'll save Lila and it will all be okay. Hades won't be too angry with me and it will all be okay. My powers will stop acting weird and I'll fight my way home and it will all. Be. Okay.

When they come into view of the courtyard, she becomes very aware that all will not be okay.

.

CHAPTER 30

There are hundreds of soldiers in rows, perhaps a thousand. They're all armed to the teeth. And even more eerie, they don't move or speak a word when they see her. Like they are expecting her.

"Stay behind me," she says to Lila.

"Persephone, I don't think this is going to work." Worry tinges her voice. Persephone has no response.

They walk until they are in view of the grand front steps, and Persephone's heart falls into her stomach. There Aetius stands, chest puffed up and a smirk on his face. And beside him stands her mother. She just looks tired. She doesn't have any reaction when she sees Persephone.

"Is that-" Lila begins.

"Yes. It is."

"Come, Persephone!" Aetius calls. "Let's have a conversation."

She doesn't move, and the arrogant smirk becomes a sneer.

"Look around. You're beat. So come up here."

Doing so would put the army in between her and the front gate, so she is not doing that. And she is not bringing Lila anywhere near him.

"You've been trying to escape, haven't you? Tried to weave your little ladders over the wall?" He tuts. "But it's not working, is it? Demeter, tell her."

"You've been doing this?" Persephone asks her mother.

"I only want you home. And safe."

"If you haven't noticed, mother, I've been shot today. By his men."

"I'm sorry. I truly am. But whatever happens up here is still safer than being down there."

"Bullshit. I can't believe you." Her voice wavers. "You would let Lila be imprisoned, starved, and who knows what else. You would let them shoot me with arrows. You wilt my attempts to escape a tyrant. As long as you get what you want."

"If you were a mother, you'd understand," Demeter says, oddly cold.

"These are not the actions of a mother," Persephone says. "They're the actions of a selfish god."

Demeter's eyes flash. "I am not *them*."

"You ARE!" Persephone screams, and it feels good. "Look around you."

"I tire of this," Aetius says. "Seize her and bring her to me."

"Unharmed, Prince?" One of the generals calls out.

Aetius shrugs. "Eh. Alive."

"No, wait!-" Demeter says, but it's too late. Every single soldier moves at once.

Persephone throws out her arms and casts a web of stems in front of her, tangling up the soldiers immediately near her, but they cut through them in a few seconds. She's panicking. There have never been this many opponents before. She shoots out bits of magic almost blindly, throwing thorns in boots and weapon hilts. A few soldiers cry out, but it's not enough to stop them completely.

"Persephone!" Demeter calls out, distracting her for a

second. Her mother is trying to work her way towards her, cutting down soldiers left and right. She does her best to ignore her and protect herself and Lila from the onslaught. If it comes down to physically fighting her mother, she's not sure she can do it.

One soldier after the other comes, and she's not proud of what she does. Thorns digging into throats, choking some until they fall back, coughing. Buds erupt from underneath their skin, causing screams of agony. She starts weeping, but they keep coming. Her power peters out little by little, until she's left with nearly nothing.

Her mother is ten feet away now. What she plans to do when she reaches Persephone, Persephone doesn't know. Men's hands reach for her and she has run out of options. They close in on her and she wants to scream in frustration, in pain, in disappointment - and then she feels a prickle alone her spine. It's akin to static electricity. She pants, closing her eyes.

"Lila, hold onto me!" She yells. And before Lila can even ask why or what, she grabs her with one arm. She feels the sky above and the breeze in her hair and the static of a storm that could come, should she wish it. And she does wish it.

She roars and squeezes her eyes shut, letting out the anger and hurt and longing and guilt. A flash of white-hot light pulses from her body.

CHAPTER 31

It knocks down every soldier and general, even her mother and the prince.
Most of them lay unconscious on the courtyard grass.
Persephone sags.

"Persephone," Lila says. She turns to see a huge portion of the wall behind them has crumbled. Beyond, they can see the forest.

"Run," Persephone whispers. "Run as far as you can. I'll make sure you're never dragged here again."

"What? You have to come with me."

"I can't, Lila." Persephone feels lightheaded, and she sways on her feet. "I'm so tired of running." *I'm so tired.*

Lila grabs her wrist and tries to tug her over to the crumbled wall, but Persephone stumbles and falls, like the rest of them.

"No, no no no. Get up!" Lila begs.

The soldiers are starting to get to their feet, dazed. Some of them do not move at all, and Persephone knows she would feel a pit in her stomach if she were not so tired. Her mother gets to her feet, a horrified expression on her face. Her hair is in disarray and she's shaking. Persephone's never seen her mother so ruffled. A few soldiers help Aetius up, and he is white faced with anger. But there's something new there -fear.

"What are you waiting for? Bring her to me." He snarls. "She's tired herself out."

Two men run over and grab her upper arms, dragging her to her feet. But they are trembling.

"Don't touch her!" Lila screams.

"Mother," Persephone calls. "If you do not get her far away from here, I will never forgive you."

Demeter is speechless. She stands, watching her daughter be dragged to the foot of the stairs. She looks haunted.

"MOTHER," Persephone screams.

Demeter winces, but strides towards Lila with purpose. "Leave, child." She says it quietly, the calm in her voice belying whatever is going on inside her.

"I can't believe you did this," Lila spits. "Look what you've done to her."

"Leave now."

"What is wrong with you?" Persephone hears Lila sob, but she can only stare at the stone before her.

Demeter summons tomato vines, almost in a daze.

"Stop. No-" Lila stutters, as they wrap around her legs and arms and drag her over the rubble. "Persephone!"

"Go far away from here," Demeter says. And once Lila is outside what used to be the wall, she brings up even more tomato vines, patching up the wall in a sort of spiky lattice so Lila can't get back inside. Lila's voice gets farther and farther away. Demeter must have her vines dragging her all the way out to the forest. Eventually, her voice falls quiet.

Demeter limps to stand beside her daughter. "Unhand her," she says to the soldiers. They look uncertainly at Aetius.

"Make her kneel," he sneers.

They shove Persephone down on her knees, and Demeter hisses, "I'll kill you."

"But you haven't yet," Aetius says, as if contemplating. "Why is that? Don't you want to have a normal life here when all this mess is over? The way things used to be? Hard to have a normal life if you kill your future king."

"But yes, be careful," Aetius says to the soldiers, sarcasm dripping from his voice. "That's no way to treat what could have been your future queen."

"I was never going to marry you." Persephone's voice is hoarse, but she can still use it.

"Not even if mommy dearest wanted you to?"

"You want me to marry him, mother?" She asks, spitting out the blood that had pooled in her mouth. It lands on his shiny boots.

"I just need you away from Hades," Demeter pleads.

"Do you want to know what he did to me? Do you even care? Aetius, I mean. Not Hades."

Her mother gets that familiar pinched expression in her face.

"He raped me," she says, at first only to her mother. Then she screams it so the whole battlefield can hear. "HE RAPED ME."

A hush falls across the courtyard. The men who were getting themselves together after being knocked on their ass go still. Aetius looks uncomfortable.

"She lies. She wanted it."

Demeter's face goes blank.

"Yes. I wanted it so bad that I stabbed you."

Demeter goes ballistic. She brings her hands up in fists and the soldiers who were holding Persephone up start choking, releasing her to claw at their throats as wheat grains tumble out of their mouths. Aetius has vines growing up his body, and he screams. They get closer and closer to his nostrils, ears, and eyes, and Persephone tries to lift herself off the ground to stop it, but she can't. No no no no. Why would her mother take this from her?

She lays her cheek on the ground beneath her. She's crying. She wants to go home, which is not even in this realm. A home that cares about her and would do anything for her. She gets deja vu. She's been in this position, in this state before. She exhales, and readies herself to use the last kernel of magic she has left. She breaks a sweat with the effort, chest heaving.

When she lifts her hand from the ground, there is a seed. She digs a hole into the earth with her fingernails. Shallow and tiny - but a bed for the seed nonetheless. She pushes the seed in the hole with her index finger and brushes dirt over top of it.

She was stupid to think she had to do this alone. She was foolish to think the only way to be strong is to be without help. She closes her eyes, and covers the little mound with her palm. She thinks of Hades. Yearns for her. Just for her arms around her and her deep laugh and dark brown eyes. Just like earth. She feels the tether between them that had gone taut when she left the underworld, tug. Like a string tied to her ribs. And then there's rushing in her ears and the ground erupts somewhere behind her. But it keeps erupting, unlike the first time.

"What-" Demeter breaths, and is distracted enough that her vines stop crawling toward Aetius's death, and the wheat grains disappear from the soldiers' lungs.

"Persephone," comes a voice that she knows as home.

CHAPTER 32

Strong hands are pulling her up, into a lap. Hades. The dreaded goddess of the underworld is sitting on the ground, cradling her. "Oh, sweetheart."

She brushes the dirt from Persephone's cheek and her jaw clenches when she sees her myriad injuries. "Oh, love."

Persephone could sob in relief. She's not mad at her. Or if she is, it's not the kind of mad that would come out in a place like this, at a time like this. It's not the kind that loves her any less.

Persephone clings to her, the part of her that usually shies away from public displays of affection gone dormant at the moment. She peeks over Hades' shoulder and sees that she's brought nearly everyone from the castle with her. They're in armor, wielding javelins and swords and bows and staffs. Some of them are empty-handed, ready to draw upon their natural powers. Sofia, Tari, Ky, Ismeni, Zina, Voleta, Minthe, and so many others that she remembers from the impromptu party the night before she left. Even Cerberus is there, looking fierce and bigger than ever.

"Why is everyone here?" She croaks.

"We were prepared for a battle, but it looks like you mostly handled it," Hades shifts her in her arms. "Can you stand?"

"I don't know."

So she gets to her feet, pulling Persephone with her. She has to support almost all of her weight, but she does so with no complaint, holding her close to her side.

"Why did you bring Hades here," Demeter asks, almost mournful. "I have it under control. I can kill him and we can be free." She gestures towards Aetius, who is trembling and white-faced on the steps. "You can come home."

"You don't get to kill him," Persephone says. "I do. I DO."

Demeter flinches back. "You can't kill him. You don't want that kind of guilt, Persephone. Let me-"

"No."

"You think you are grown enough to understand what it takes to kill-"

"STOP," Persephone yells. "STOP TELLING ME WHO I AM AND WHAT TO DO."

Demeter's mouth hangs open.

Hades helps her walk up the stairs to stand in front of her mother.

"If he's dead, he can't hurt anyone else ever again. If I feel guilty later, I'll deal with it. But I'm not the only person who needs him gone."

She and Hades go to stand over Aetius, who has stood up now and is trying to hedge against the wall as inconspicuous as possible.

"I'm sorry, Persephone," He stutters. "I swear."

"You're not. And even if you were, I still wouldn't be able to forgive you. I *hate* you, do you understand me?"

He looks like he may cry. "So what will you do to me?"

When she sees him, she sees the face of Maisie, of Lila, of the gaunt prisoners in the dungeons. She sees her own face, the carefree little girl she used to be, the angry young woman she became. She sees the countless times she turned away from her own reflection. The countless other girls who might have done the same. And though he cowers against a cold stone wall, and she does feel a bit guilty for making another human being afraid, she forces herself to remember that he would not give it a second thought if their current positions were reversed. That he forced himself upon her and others and would do so again, if allowed to go on. He felt he was entitled to her body, to hurt her body. To give himself gratification in the act of hurting her. To ruin her life. He would never understand the scope of what he's done.

"Nothing worse than what you've done to me."

She stops closer to him and grabs his jaw so that he must look her in the face. The terror and the hatred she sees in his eyes pleases her immensely. Hades squeezes her hip and she feels a low roll of power from her goddess crash over her, if something could crash softly. Somehow, she is giving her a bit of her power, or energy. Something.

So Persephone grabs onto that bit of something with all her might, and she calls to the earth beneath them and the life that grows there, and she wills it inside of Aetius's body. She plants coriander in his eye sockets, foxglove in his throat, and marigold in his heart. She watches as the roots grow through his eyes, so similar to veins, and then the little white petals burst open so you can no longer see the gore beneath it. She watches him choke and try to scream and the stems climb their way over his tongue and then bloom outside his lips, tiny purple bells spilling out over his chin. He slides to the floor, a writhing mass of flesh. The marigolds push through his chest and shirt, bright orange and scarlet, so that the red of his blood merely blends in with the sunset blooms. He twitches and gasps and scratches his face and chest. The sounds he makes are horrid. Pitiful. It tears at her heart and is music to her ears all at once.

After a minute or so of his agony, Persephone kneels

down and pulls out the bouquet of marigolds from his heart - bits of the organ clinging to the roots. He stops moving. The blood pools out from his body. He's close enough to the edge that it spills over, drip, drip dripping down the steps. His golden hair is mussed, sharp blue eyes bloodshot and unseeing.

She gazes at his mangled body. The silence of it all.

Hades presses a kiss to her temple.

YOUR EYES AS HONEY

YOUR EYES AS HONEY

YOUR EYES AS HONEY

A dead body is a horrible thing. The act of killing someone, even more horrible. But as she clutches the flowers in her fist, all she feels is stillness.

YOUR EYES AS HONEY

CHAPTER 33

"Persephone?" Hades whispers her name gently.

She looks over to her, this beautiful goddess of a woman that loves her so. All she wants at this moment is to sit in her warm bathtub and not come out for a very, very long time.

Her voice is quiet when she asks, "Can we go home now?" *Is it over? Please let it all be over.*

Hades nods, still supporting her as they turn to the steps. A sea of people stares up at them.

None of the soldiers attempt to apprehend her again. They stand, solemn and silent. Hades' people do too, and she has a split second of worry that they are judging her, will not accept her after this. But she catches eyes with Ky and they nod to her, eyes filled with understanding. Solidarity.

They begin down the steps into the courtyard, but she stops midway, turning to look at her mother. Demeter has a look of heartbreak, of devastation.

"You hid my power, somehow, didn't you? Or tried to suppress it."

Her mother's mouth opens, and closes. Demeter's voice trembles when she says, "Persephone, I never wanted to hurt you." She is crying. It's the first time Persephone thinks she's seen her mother cry. It's jarring, and Persephone feels the stirrings of the young girl who would do anything to make her mother happy again, despite the betrayal and loss and the chaos of what just happened. She wonders if that will ever go away.

Demeter's words are all the confirmation Persephone needs. She tugs on Hades' sleeve so they can continue on their way home. Demeter doesn't call after her.

They board Hades' chariot, and the earth takes them back below. The rest of their people follow, some shadow-hopping like Hades and others boarding their own chariots.

They land on the castle lawn in darkness, like the first time Persephone was here. Once her foot touches the ground the sun peeks over the horizon, faster than normal.

"We're happy to have you back, princess," Minthe says, touching her shoulder as she passes. It seems the realm itself is, too, if the speedy sunrise is any indication.

Persephone is relieved to walk the halls of this castle again, even with its cold, damp corners and drafts, it still feels full of life. Cozy. Like her very bones know she's home. Hades takes her straight to her bedroom, which might as well be theirs now for she has no intention of leaving it for the foreseeable future. Once the door closes behind them, Hades gathers her in her embrace, tight and warm and fierce. Persephone presses her face in the crook of her neck and clings to her.

"I'm sorry," she says.

Hades shushes her.

"You're not going to fuss at me for leaving?"

"I think you've gone through enough today. Maybe later."

Persephone exhales. "You're too good for me." There's heartache in her voice. It's a sad fact she's admitting to them both.

Hades pulls back to look at her, frowning. "Don't say that, don't ever say that." She shakes her head. "You're the best thing in my life."

Persephone looks away from her intensity, and she takes the opportunity to kiss her temple. "You make absolutely no sense to me sometimes," Hades murmurs against her hair.

She has to take a few breaths through her nose to keep from crying for the umpteenth time. "I'm going to take a bath," she says. "I'll be out in a bit."

Hades nods. "I'll be here."

Persephone takes the longest bath she's ever taken in her life. She doesn't put in any of the special oils or flowers that are stocked, just hot water. She takes the time alone to process what happened - what she made happen.

A part of her feels guilty, yes. The part that was taught in school that violence was never the answer, and killing someone bad made you just as bad as them. But a larger part of her feels relief knowing he is gone, and some measure of satisfaction from being the one to do it. What they don't teach you in schools is that some men are worse than monsters, she thinks. Yes they may have mothers that love them and friends and hobbies and may even perform acts of kindness, but when they do something as horrible as what Aetius did to her and others, she believes almost no punishment would be too much. All of the old adages and fables say only love can cure evil. But what she did does feel like an act of love, in a way. Not for him, but for herself and the other women. And it did in fact cure that particular evil.

She weeps, nonetheless. And by the time she decides she's done weeping, she feels only a bit more settled in her body.

She comes out wrapped in a towel to find Hades sitting in one of the chairs by the fire, a spread of all her favorite foods on the table. She's set out clothes on the bed for her as well, her favorite robe and Hades' shirt, knit socks and undies. Persephone dons them all and goes to her, and Hades brushes Persephone's hair while she eats. The bread rolls seem to be more buttery than usual, fluffier. Or maybe it's just because this morning she wasn't sure if she'd live to ever have another.

Persephone crawls up into her lap when she's done, Hades' palm stroking lazy lines from her knee to her thigh as they watch the flames dance in the fireplace. It soothes Persephone so much that she falls asleep with her head on Hades' shoulder.

CHAPTER 34

Persephone wakes up some measure of time later, when Hades stands with her in her arms and walks over to the bed. She sets her down among the blankets and pillows, but she doesn't get on the bed with her. Persephone sits up, cross-legged, looking up at her.

"You're very mad at me, aren't you," she says, anxious to get this over with. Her hands clasps each other tightly in her lap, and she can feel them turning white.

"Never do something like that again," Hades says. "You terrified me. I woke up and you weren't there and I couldn't feel you anywhere in this realm." she starts pacing. "And just as I alerted everyone, I heard you calling me. And I arrive to find you nearly dead."

She doesn't even raise her voice, but Persephone still feels the urge to cry anyway. But she's done enough of that recently, so she instead stares at the laces of Hades' shirt.

"You have *no* idea how terrified I was," she says.

"I'm sorry." And Persephone is. She really, really is. Hades deserves so much. She doesn't want to be someone who hurts people she loves.

"Just tell me why, please. Did you not trust me?"

"I thought the only way I could do it was alone. And

you said it yourself that if you thought I was in danger you would interfere."

"Why did you think you had to do it alone? Why are you willing to put yourself in danger like that?"

"It's how it's always been," she says, shrugging. "I don't think I know how to be not alone."

"But you had people. You had Lila, your mother-"

"I didn't have Lila like that. In the end, she still left me. And even when she was around, I felt like if she knew everything about me she wouldn't love me. The same with my mother."

"Do you feel like that about me?"

"Sometimes."

"And that's why you wouldn't let me help you?"

"I did let you, eventually."

"Persephone."

She nods. "I think so." Her voice is small, and she stares at her hands.

"Fine."

She hears Hades moving and for a moment she's terrified that she's walking out of the room, but she feels hands on her thighs and then she's moving - Hades has pulled her to the edge of the bed so her legs dangle off. She gets on her knees in between them. It would be a scandalous position if it weren't for the serious look in her eye. It's different to have Hades be the one looking up at her. Her hands rest on Persephone's hips and she gazes at her, almost supplicant.

"Tell me all the things you think make you unlovable."

"What?"

"You heard me."

"I… I don't think I can."

"You can. Tell me one thing."

Persephone thinks, but it's hard with Hades' hands on her, chest bracketed between her calves. "I'm a mean person sometimes. Most of the time."

"I haven't found that to be true in my experience, but

even if you have been mean, I know you are a good person. And if you aren't a good person? I still want you. If you're not a good person, then I'm not either, and we can rot together in mean-spiritedness for eternity."

She looks at her sharply. "You're a very good person."

Hades just raises her eyebrow in a pointed manner.

"I don't think that's how it's supposed to be," Persephone says. "You're supposed to want a good person, and want to be good."

"Do you want to be good?"

"Very much so," she says. *Desperately*. "Don't you?"

"I want to be good, I suppose. But I want you more."

She has no answer for that, but selfish relief. She's a bit confused by the conversation but Hades is still here, still holding her. And that's more than she feels she deserves.

"So what else?" Hades asks.

"I can be selfish. And manipulative."

"Okay. I still want you."

"I am judgmental, and jealous, and annoying."

"Still love you."

Persephone feels a bizarre mix of frustration and relief rise in her and she huffs, "I'm just not someone I want to be around."

"Well that's your loss, because I do."

She groans, putting her face in her hands.

"You're not going to convince me to hate you," Hades says, and wraps her arms around Persephone so she can press a kiss to her sternum.

"Do you want to know the truth? You can be all those things, and still be the brave, kind, passionate, witty girl I know you to be."

It feels like the breath has been knocked out of her. It can't be true, can it? "I don't know what to do with that," she says.

"Just keep it."

Persephone puts her palms on either side of Hades' face, tracing her cheekbone with a thumb. "I don't know what I'd do without you," she says, because they're being honest.

"You would make it. You're strong," Hades replies, turning her head to kiss Persephone's palm. It dawns on Persephone then that for all her love and acceptance of her, Hades doesn't quite understand the necessity of herself. She'll have to work on that, she decides. But all she can do at the moment is shake her head, thread her fingers through her goddess's hair, and kiss her deeply.

CHAPTER 35

Months later, the castle's back garden has tripled in size. It resembles more of a jungle than a garden, with all the growth Persephone has planted. Hades is working right now, but she usually comes out there to find her before dinner. The place bursts with color, the sun shining down and bouncing off the streams and fountains and little waterfalls. In the way back, there is a clearing. Persephone lies in it. Her eyes closed, her breathing even. She is not sleeping, but rather listening. The buzz of bees, conversations among warblers and shrikes, the gentle shush of the creek in the forest. Calendula, Anthemis, and Chrysanthemum tickle her face. The sun soaks into her skin, warming her until she feels like a band of light. Her whole body hums.

YOUR EYES AS HONEY

ABOUT THE AUTHOR

This is the first book Kate Holloway has ever written. It's not perfect, she says, but she had a hell of a time writing it, and she hopes you had a hell of a time reading it. She lives with her roommates and two cats in some southern town in some southern state.